Inside Out: Intimate Voices Stories

Inside Out: Intimate Voices
Stories

By Irene Cairo

International Psychoanalytic Books (IPBooks)
New York • http://www.IPBooks.net

Inside Out: Intimate Voices Stories

Published by IPBooks, Queens, NY
Online at: www.IPBooks.net

Cover artwork: *"Una Tarde con Jorge Luis."*
                        Reproduced with permission by the artist.
                        Gabriela Aberastury, 2021

ISBN 978-1-956864-33-5

Table of Contents

INTRODUCTION

The best short story writers engage you in a way that makes you, without realizing it, eager to learn what will happen next—and then, ultimately, surprise you. Irene Cairo is one of them. Her stories are page turners. They're suspenseful, but not because they are action packed in the traditional sense. They move right along, partly because of the fluidity of Cairo's prose and partly because of her wonderful ear for internal monologue. Her characters narrate experiences of life situations, ordinary and extraordinary; and because their narratives are so psychologically true, the tensions, the dynamism, the drama of experience emerges. It emerges organically. There's nothing in the least contrived about Cairo's stories, despite the fact that the reader is invariably set up for the unexpected—the unexpected that leaves you thinking.

Fair warning: This is the kind of book you pick up at bedtime, thinking that you will read one story before going to sleep, and then stay up far too late because you just can't stop!

Owen Renik

WAITING FOR VERMEER

She saw the line went around Constitution Avenue and Kenny said, oh my God, we got past it, the end must be on the other side. They all ran to the end and sure enough, the end was now on Seventh. A man and a woman in bright yellow slickers were running too and they got there first. I ate too much breakfast she thought quite incongruously. What if these two idiots are the last ones to get in? They all stood in the drizzle, opened the umbrellas and peered ahead.

When she had awakened that morning it was still dark, but maybe it was not so early, perhaps it was dark because of the storm. The feeling in her stomach was familiar, before the ideas could get organized and clear; when they did, the sick, empty feeling descended into her pelvis and at the same time rose to her throat. With her mouth almost opened, she heard herself moan. But then unexpectedly she let out a laugh, mercilessly, as Kenny's face appeared on her mind. I feel the same as when mother died, she thought, how absurd can I be, how pathetic? Ah, but she had been young then, and though her friends said, too young to lose her mother, at nineteen, she had the unending energy of youth, the confidence, the arrogance almost. And losing one's parents was a *natural* thing after all, something that sooner or later happened to *everybody*. In fact it happened sometimes to young children, like in all the books she loved, specially as a child, David Copperfield, Jane Eyre, where orphans could endure terrible hardship but in the end, in the end they were rewarded with love. LOVE. That was the ultimate prize, it didn't matter how much you had suffered with horrible stepparents or assorted mean relatives, sadistic principals or nasty envious children, in the end you were a better person for it, and you met a wonderful friendly thoughtful caring person —someone you could be caring, friendly, wonderful to. Usually you didn't know right from the beginning this was to be your true love, but in the end it would all be revealed. Victorian rewards of love, to the just and to the caring. So she had endured her mother's death. Everybody lost parents, sooner or later, but everybody found love, yes, first they suffered disappointments sure, took wrong paths, were mistreated, they could be shy like Jane Eyre, rebels like Jo Marsh, or, as her literary tastes evolved, even lame like Philip Carey. There had been more losses in her life, though, and last year, her father had the stroke, the horrible stroke. She had realized quickly that being an only child had that awful price tag, you had to go through all these things alone, and make decisions. But Kenny, as usual, had come to her help. There was always that tender unspoken sexiness between them, but this time besides advising her on what decisions to make, as far as the doctors, the kind of care, which institution to choose, all of those steps now looming for her, when he had left, he had kissed her on the lips, as usual, but this time he had lingered, and he had pressed her against him. In January he had come down specially from Boston to help her find a place. Because he had been a medic in the Army and because of his sophistication about everything else, she knew he would know what questions to ask the doctors and what place to select. It was after that trip that things had seemed so much clearer to her. He loves me, for sure, she had felt. But he is so thoughtful, he knows I am going through such a stressful moment. He wouldn't want me to feel too overwhelmed, and surely, he would not want to cloud our romance with the sadness of the decisions about my father. What if not love would make a man come down from Boston to D.C., to help a woman arrange for her father's nursing home? A man in Academia, a tenured professor of English Literature, 38, divorced, attractive, bright, a great skier, a great tennis player. Why would he spend a whole weekend with her, doing awful things like looking at hospitals and nursing homes, unless he truly loved her? But was it possible? She had considered herself coldly: I am 35, never married, very slightly overweight, my skin may be lovely but my teeth are a little crooked… but I have great lips they say and I have learned to smile so the lips show more and the teeth less.

So in January she was almost sure. More than after previous trips. The other times he had come for Visiting Lecturer stuff, he always stayed at her place, he brought her flowers, bought wine, he lit candles when she made dinner . He kissed her lightly, sometimes not so lightly, when he left. They talked on the phone all the time, he inquired about all the things that were important to her. He ended each call with a sweet, "love yeah".

It had been his idea to come to see the Vermeer show, because although the show was completely sold out there were a few same day tickets. We'll get up really early on Saturday, he said, and stand in line, we'll get in, I am sure. They had set the date. On Friday early morning—he usually took the Friday 6 P.M. Shuttle—he had called: Francine, baby, would it be all right if I brought a friend who would *really love* to see the show? A friend? She had repeated stupidly. She had planned a romantic dinner, had bought a Vermeer catalog as a present for him, "in case we slept late on Saturday", she had planned to say coyly. A friend? I only have one guest room, she had added. There had been this imperceptible silence. He could sleep on the sofa, Ken had said. At least it's a he- friend, she breathed to herself. For a moment she had been scared, feeling it was too good to be true, another woman's got him. Now she felt, Ken is so generous, some friend wants to see the Vermeer show, he offers them a place in Washington. My place.

The couple ahead, who had run ahead of them, were in active conversation with the group ahead of them, they were talking about chances. Chances to get in. The couple in yellow slickers were obviously foreigners, although they spoke good English. The group ahead of those two were much younger, they were the ones who did most of the talking; one young man might be a College student. They had been there the previous weekend, and their place in line was much farther ahead, and yet they had not gotten in. The foreign woman in the yellow slicker said: but maybe they had previously sold more tickets for that day; foreign man chirped in: you can never tell from those kinds of things. Francine found that despite the fact they had run ahead, she liked their optimism. She had closed the umbrella because the rain seemed to have stopped but now it was starting again, and harder. Foreign woman had done the same, she now turned and looked at Francine and as they both opened their umbrellas again foreign woman in yellow slicker said, we were too optimistic, maybe if we keep the umbrella open no matter what, the rain will stop. Francine found that further, surprisingly, she liked her craziness. The woman looked straight into her eyes, and Francine saw her look at Ken, busily talking to Alejandro at that moment, and again at her; she had the crazy notion that this foreign woman with the strange beautiful green eyes took it all in and figured it out. She looked kind, and thoughtful. Francine felt like crying again. Well, certainly *I* could not figure it out. I *still* cannot figure it out, she thought.

Usually Ken rented a car at National Airport every time he came in. She didn't have a car and living on Dupont Circle didn't miss it. They had arrived at her house around nine. He had made the introductions. My friend, Alejandro Diaz Escobar, he is Mexican. Alejandro was gorgeous. He spoke perfect English. It turned out he was studying at Harvard. He seemed younger than the two of them but the conversation had been easy. Already on the phone Ken had insisted that she shouldn't cook and they should go out. They had come back quite late, and had brandy, as they always did when they were alone. Finally she had said, I'll get the linen for the sofa. The two men had looked at each other and Ken had said, it's perfectly O.K. as it is, Alejandro can just sleep on it, with a blanket maybe. She had laughed, strangely anxious, don't be ridiculous! She had brought the linen, began to open the sofa, although they stopped her, and Ken had finished making the bed.

Now foreign woman turned back to her, they had been in animated conversation with the other group, and announced: those two are leaving, apparently, they were standing in line for a friend, and they decided to go get *croissants* instead. Francine laughed: I don't think they really were into it, she said, the young man didn't seem enthusiastic about this thing. Foreign man turned too, and addressed Ken and Alejandro saying: two less, it's better for all of us. Suddenly they were all talking, foreign couple were voluble, happy, told the whole story of their lives. They were Chilean exiles. They now lived in New York, because after the murder of Letelier they had decided they would never live in Washington. Suddenly foreign man and Alejandro were speaking Spanish. Was it her imagination or they were lowering their voices? They were forming a little circle of their own. Foreign woman, Ken, and herself were drawn into this wider circle, but Ken was very near her body. She felt like crying again. Foreign woman took a glance towards her husband, it was her husband, that was clear in the *we* they used, and then looked at Ken and Francine: you two don't speak Spanish I guess, she affirmed. No, they answered. For a moment she thought THANK GOD! Thank God Ken doesn't speak Spanish. Though maybe it would be different in a different way. Maybe there would be no mystery, no exotic aspects to Alejandro. She stopped herself, here I am… guessing what I do not want to know… Foreign woman declared, I am soo hungry, we left with only coffee, I thought there would be some entrepreneurial crew selling food alongside the line, in New York there would be. Kenny looked at the woman and then at Francine, there was something conspiratorial in his look. I have an apple, Francine revealed. Foreign woman looked amazed, and then when Francine produced the apple and started to slice it with a Swiss Army knife she opened those green eyes even wider: are you sure you want to share it? Yes, I am sure, she said, I already had breakfast. She passed slices of apple around and foreign husband and Alejandro also took some and then continued in their *tete a tete.*

Foreign wife said: Thanks! I feel rejuvenated, I am going to walk around to look at what's happening up front, maybe we can find out what our prospects are. As soon as she left Ken leaned gently towards her, whispering: how are you doing? I am a little wet she answered evasively, and I could be warmer. Alejandro turned back to them: you know these people have been to Mexico every year, they have a house in Zihuatanejo. Foreign husband added: but we also have been all over Mexico, Mexico has always been good to exiles, we love Mexico, have you two been? Ken answered no at the same time that she said yes. She fell silent again. When foreign wife returned, she reported that there had been some further progress in the line. And indeed in a few seconds they started inching forward slowly, sinuously. Now foreign couple sounded cheery.

How can I endure this? Francine wondered, one shock after another. I'm still reeling. How will I live through this? Who am I? What do I convey to other people? Where was I? Where was I ?!

She screamed internally, full of rage now. Rage that she had kept so quietly locked, rage she had not known until now. But, her reasonable voice emerged again, once again, like it had so many times before in her life, maybe he is right!!! Maybe Kenny is right in some way, maybe he knows something that I don't. Dramatic questions, vivid memories started to turn vertiginously in her mind. what about that kiss, what about your body pressing against mine, what about… She thought she might have sobbed out loud, because of the look on foreign woman's face…Her beautiful eyes looked so kind … That kindness had the potential to bring her to the verge of tears.

Francine dear, Ken had said in the morning, we are too much alike, we are like siblings.. We could never… be together that way…It's.. it would be… incestuous in a way…

Incestuous!!! And she had not dared ask him directly about Alejandro, not the question she really had in mind…

Is it me making wrong choices? She thought of Ted, the three years of waiting for him to get the divorce he claimed he was eager to get… She thought of the clandestine relationship with Russ. If her mother had not already been dead, it would have killed her. And, she certainly could not have introduced a black man to her father. But then she started therapy and she was confident she was on the right path.

A car slowed down and a man in the back seat rolled down the window and called out to them.

Alejandro and foreign husband walked out to the curb, and chatted a few moments, then came back. Tourists, they explained, they wanted to know what is going on with this line... Foreign husband then said " I wonder where they are from ... but what would they think if they knew, and if not, what would they think about all of us? We are here because of an only moderately successful Dutch painter from the 17th Century who died leaving his family in debt... "

Francine thought of the two of them, foreign couple... actually, now she knew from where, Chilean couple, Chilean exiles. Obviously higher education, obviously sophisticated, obviously curious, engaged, and warm...

Do you do this often? She found herself asking the wife out loud.

Do what? Stand in line in the rain to see a show? Francine chuckled... they all chuckled. Then she answered... *We met in the first year of University. There was going to be a lecture on the DNA sequence by somebody important, some American close to the Nobel Prize, it was so crowded, I was in danger of being trampled...Jose Luis looked at me , sheltered me and helped me get in .. So, yes it's clearly a bad habit to be in crowds.... we have been together ever since...*

They all were smiling now. Francine included. The tenderness that now had been evoked in her by this story covered the bitterness that she had been struggling with.

Now that "Jose Luis" had emerged… they all exchanged names.

The Chileans talked about political meetings in Chile… Other bits and pieces emerged…

No, no, we didn't live together until we were married. You don't do that where we come from…

She smiled as she said that…

Gradually, slowly, Francine began to imagine the story… The love story…Together in University, together through good and bad… Why could that not happen to her?

Well, she had to admit it was too late in her life for such a story…

Somehow, however, strangely, mysteriously, the story had taken her rage away…

As the relief swept over her, they detected a commotion ahead. People turned, yelled, gesticulated. "Nobody else today!"

So, they chatted some more, told of their plans, the Chilean couple said they would go back to their hotel and then decide what to do…

Ken, Alejandro and her were let in a small circle.

Ken looked at her, seemingly with great concern. Francine, Alejandro has never been to the Air and Space, why don't we go? I know you have been but….

Don't worry she interrupted, don't worry, definitely, go ahead, I have my own plans…

There was some resistance, but she was so clear and appeared so tranquil, they finally accepted. They would meet back at her place and decide on dinner later.

Once the two of them left in the direction of the Smithsonian, she began to walk, thinking, perhaps I can go to the Museum of the American Indian and think of people who have suffered more… She realized she was returning to her biting, self mocking style…

The wind picked up and she struggled with the umbrella, her old small traveling umbrella which seemed on the verge of breaking.

As she did face the wind, a tall man passed by and asked, do you need help with that? No, she said, I am sure I can manage, this umbrella still has life in it… She smiled reassuringly to the kind face towering over her…

The kind face said: You know, I am sure you did not notice me but I was on the line standing behind you, I was alone so I could overhear your talking…

I myself am South American, so I guess that made me focus on you all.

You mentioned you are an anthropologist. I hope you don't think I am impertinent, but I am going to go for the first time to the Museum of the American Indian… Are you by any chance interested in going? It would be great to have a knowledgeable "guide".

Francine was stunned. No, no, I am not crazy she thought, I know nobody reads minds. And I know this is not some Pinochet inspired plot either…Her wild thoughts made her smile again, involuntarily.

You have a lovely smile the kind tall man said, does that mean yes?

Well, Francine answered slowly… I do not mind… I love that Museum….

BREAST BIOPSY

I can't take my eyes off the rings. From time to time I raise my gaze up to the face to answer an insistent question when it is repeated in the same soap opera voice, but mostly I just stare at the rings, and away from her boobs, and have to keep making an effort to direct my eyes anywhere else.

We sit across from one another in the little cubicle of the Admissions office. I can't quite absorb the rhythm of the questions interspersed with her chatter: "Your husband is on the staff, is that right? Your Social Security number is…?" I answer yes, pause, and then the number. The mixed rhythm goes on, as she looks at the monitor and then at me, ready with the next question, the singsong of her chatter grating my ears, her multi-ringed fingers never leaving the keyboard. "You still at the same address on East 65th Street? That's a pretty sweater you are wearing, isn't it lovely outside, really spring… did you by any chance knit that yourself? It is so-oh pretty, it does seem handmade, they don't make things like that anymore these days, your telephone number is still 734-9976?"

Yes same address, yes truly spring, no I didn't make it myself but it is handmade. Despite myself, with shame I volunteer the name of the store, infected by her tone and perhaps also because I'm so anxious, despite all the reassurance, despite Jim's words on the phone, yesterday twice, this morning at six—for him it was 3 A.M. He did say to call him before I left the house. Yes, the same phone number.

When she introduced herself and told me she was going to fill in the admission sheet, I thought she looked like a movie character, somebody's imagination of a jazz singer, huge, tall, bosomy, so bosomy! Huge boobs, why did this have to happen to me TODAY, I thought, not yet knowing what was to come. Wonderful contralto voice, chocolaty shiny skin, the huge jewelry, BIG pendant between the BIG boobs, and above everything else, the rings on every finger except the thumbs, huge stones, a lot of silver; in my deranged mind I reached for wit, I thought; it's a collection taken from all the victims, the women who didn't make it. She is Charon on my way to Hell...

Christine came with me this morning. It was Jim's suggestion—so he could feel less guilty I'm certain—but I would have thought of it anyway when I felt resigned and knew for sure that he was not coming back for today. I first tried to think that I could go through this alone, but I was feeling so forlorn, and Christine is a great friend and she offered and even insisted. They want you to have somebody pick you up anyway, she said. She also said she'd bring a book and wait through the procedure and then take me home.

I spent a fortune in phone calls just in the last two days. When Jim first got the news about his mother ten days ago, we debated if I should go too. I didn't really want to, but I volunteered, as usual. No, no, I doubt she'll recognize anybody, even me, Jim's words made sense and he didn't have to say what we both knew, that if she did recognize me, it would not make her last few hours easier. Only twenty-two years of marriage and three grandchildren she truly does love, but she still does not think her son should have married me.

We sat over breakfast before I was to take him to the airport. Weeks earlier I had scheduled the mammogram for the next morning. Could you wait until after tomorrow, I had asked. Don't be ridiculous, he had answered, as I knew he would, It's a mammogram, for God's sake, it's not even an invasive procedure! You know how I get though, I had added plaintively, hopelessly. Yes of course I know how you get, he had been tender despite the words that followed, how you get… crazy, despite all those years on a couch… It does not make a poor ignorant surgeon like me believe in psychoanalysis; you better not let your friends know and just get some Valium. He had made it much softer then by leaning over the breakfast table and kissing me right on the mouth, a kiss from the old days, forceful and passionate. I knew he meant it too. He meant even more what he said next, Marianne, baby, we would both feel pretty awful if I stayed for your routine mammogram and she died tomorrow. I too meant what I said next, in my meanest sarcastic tone. With luck she'll die right after you arrive —he started to laugh—and you can come back on the red-eye tonight and you can let Ronnie make the funeral arrangements.

He laughed. I can always make him laugh with the most outrageous things. We both know that Ronnie is helpless. Ronnie, husband number three, knows it too, and he never expected this. Nor did anyone else. She had already buried two husbands, Jim's father, who was a real prince, like my Jim, and then Samuel who everybody thought was already dead when she married him. They probably fixed something funny between them against his children and she got most of the money. Then came Ronnie, who thought he was checking into a luxury resort for his last few years, which was all he wanted; that was exactly right for him, a woman to take care of everything. He didn't expect her to have this kind of massive stroke; not only could he not be expected to take care of funeral arrangements, he could not arrange to get her to the hospital, speak to doctors, make decisions! Jim is not only the only son; he is HER SON THE DOCTOR. Ronnie had called but she would have summoned Jim without words. I think she knew telepathically I had scheduled a mammogram, and worse! She knew it would not be "routine," she knew they would find that funny little calcification, she wanted me to sweat it out alone, without Jim, her last laugh, she dies in California while I long for my Jim in New York, and he is there WITH HER. She never liked younger people in general. Now she is taking my Jimmy away from me as she takes her time dying. And Ronnie, who was ready to go first, poor soul, who will control his life now? Jim says he is destroyed. She is taking her sweet time, but in the meantime, unbelievably, she does not recognize anybody, she can't say anything but she spoke Jim's name! One week already that he has been there! Now they say it's a matter of hours… for seven days already!

This is all deserved and there is going to be worse punishment, for my being so cruel and outspoken. She has sent me this curse, from coast to coast; the biopsy will be positive, or else, more ironic, I will die on the table, alone, the first woman to die of shock from a breast biopsy! At least I will make a headline. I must have been convincing in my terror—which was quite genuine—because after Jim spoke to my surgeon on the phone, with me already having apparently agreed that it was ridiculous to wait and be more anxious, I called Dr. Petersen again and he said, "You know Marianne, if you are *that* frightened we *could* wait until Jim comes back."

Wildly I thought: he is afraid too, he knows a patient like me can die on the table, I can die of fright, he does not want to be sued, he does not want a staff surgeon's wife to die in his hands. Terror had oozed from my voice, Dr. Petersen are YOU telling me to wait? "No, I am not telling you to wait; it makes more sense to do it now, it will be all right. Actually, if it wasn't because of your family history, we would not even do it now, we'd wait six months, repeat the mammogram and see. This way we'll do it in the morning and we'll probably know in the afternoon and everything will be fine. This way it will be over with." We had been through the same dialogue already; I thought I must try to be rational.

Miss Rings interrupts my thoughts, as she types and types. "Oh, you are a psychologist !!! A Ph.D., I see here, is that some kind of a doctor too?" Not the same kind of doctor, yes a psychologist. "OOOH, Hooow In-ter-es-ting! And I keep calling you Mrs.! I should call you Doctor! And tell me Doctor, I am very curious, do you specialize in anything?" Thoughts of death, I answer silently. Yes, adolescents, I say out loud. "REALLY? You know, I almost went into social work, I am a foster parent for the City. I have kept so many children!" Reflexively, my eyes go back to the rings, I can't help it. Maybe the rings belonged to the mothers, another wild thought, but consistent with my generally deranged state of mind. "Oh DOCTOR, I can't believe this coincidence ! You know I have been thinking for months, for MONTHS of consulting a specialist in adolescents..." She is breathless, perhaps from the effort to speak one sentence without chanting. My eyebrows must have gone up, fast, luckily before I have time to ask, stupidly, "For you?" She reads my eyebrows though, and laughs, "No, not for me Doctor, I am well past that age, but I had a TERRIBLE experience, you know! I was so upset…. I don't need any aggravation… You know it is very hard to be a foster parent," (breathless, with that contralto voice) "now I am facing a hearing, it is AWFUL. Do you have Major Medical? Or Wraparound?" What?!!! Oh God, …I don't really know, it's my husband's plan… Whatever you all have here… "OH! We don't ALL have the same insurance, Doctor, don't you have your card?" I feel more like an idiot by the minute. Yes, yes of course I have my card…here, Wraparound Plus. "I see, of course, Doctor, it is the best plan, absolutely the best, you may choose one of three plans, Doctor, this is the best…" She looks at the card, types… "Well, last year I had this foster child, Jesse, he had been in some trouble himself, but I thought the real problem was the family. I always have boys, I prefer boys, they are really less trouble, I see you have three children, boys or girls?" She smiles. Two girls one boy I say softly. It's bad enough that we have to talk at all, I think, it's bad enough that she can ask me about my life and say something about my Jim, talk about my profession, know my address and phone number, but to mention anything connected with my children seems to me ominous. Apocalyptic thoughts have invaded my brain. I think the Fates are against me, my

Jimmy away, next to his dying mother, while I am having a breast biopsy for the first time in my life. The first, ha, ha, ha, the savage audience interrupts, the first! You think there will be many? You are already bargaining with God, aren't you Marianne, the first! Indeed, you are trying to imagine you will grow old, there will be many, you will get used to them. If it wasn't for your family history, says Dr. Petersen's voice… Do not mention my children, I pray internally, in terror. Dear God: even if I die on the operating table, God, protect my children… "OH, TWO girls and a boy, how lovely, I hope you are not offended, Doctor, girls can be lovely, I am sure, but they are more work, don't you think, I mean you have to watch them much more, don't you? Well, that's what I had always thought, but after this experience I myself don't know, that's why I have to ask a professional… Let me get these other papers ready, you are going to have to sign some things… Well, I get this boy placed as a foster child," she lowers her voice to near a whisper, "his name is Jesse, he seems nice, he is shy, fourteen-years old you see. And they have to report to a counselor periodically and for me it's routine, but this time I get a letter from the City…"

I want to disconnect. Oh God, help me! My thoughts are running wild and I am trying to soothe myself remembering Jim's voice on the phone in phone call number forty-three probably, two days ago, once we had scheduled this thing…

How can you not be with me, I was almost crying, what's the use of being married to a surgeon if he is not there when you need him? He had then said gently, I would laugh if it didn't hurt your feelings right now. Laugh, yes, laugh, what am I going to do with my wedding band, for instance? He had been quiet for a moment. I knew we both had thought the exact same thing, we had been transported twenty years back, there were only a few minutes left before that other surgery, we knew it was an ectopic pregnancy, I had given him my wedding band, and trying not to cry had whispered, "You keep it, you, you, you understand? Only you, and if…You know, I hate to take it off…But if I….if I don't … Jim, you slip it back on my finger as soon as I come out of the O.R., but if I…" He had leaned over then and kissed me then, shut me up, then. No ifs, he had said, no ifs, I know it will be all right, don't be frightened, no ifs, I'll slip it back on as soon as you come out, I'll be waiting. And then he had held me tight, very tight, and said between his teeth, I don't care about the baby, I don't care, I only care about you… And I had gone into the O.R., and gone under, holding on to those words, and sure enough when I had come out of the O.R. I must have looked like death, and was too weak to say anything, but as they wheeled me out I had managed to lift my left hand and as he ran next to my stretcher being wheeled wildly through the corridors he had slipped my wedding band back on, smiling, and I had looked at his smile and into his eyes and said, But I lost the baby and the tube, didn't I? Marianne baby, I don't care, he had said, I don't care.

So, time passed, we were lucky… and we have three beautiful children.

He said the right things then… But now is now, so the day before yesterday I asked him on the phone, What if they have to take off my breast? They won't, he said. But what if they have to? I had insisted, you will not like me with one breast … Miss Rings' deep voice, relentlessly, "I get this letter from the City and they tell me to come in for an appointment, imagine Doctor, I come and they put me alone in a room and make me wait and then this Supervisor comes and looks at me kind of funny, and says, you know, Jesse is saying these things, don't you have anything to tell me? And DOCTOR! I have no idea what he is talking about, and I say so! And then …just a minute, here, sign this form here, that's right, thank you, Doctor, I will call the floor and then I will get someone to take you upstairs… So he insists: are you sure? With this funny expression… Well Doctor, my word of honor…and then he looks at me and says: Jesse says… these things about you. And I ask WHAT!" For a moment she looks straight into my eyes, puts her hands on the table, imitating herself, "WHAT does he say about me? I ask. And the supervisor says, Jesse says that you asked him, Doctor you could not IMAGINE! My heart was beating so fast but I didn't really expect it, Doctor, I swear, you'll have to tell me if adolescents can be like this, Doctor, the supervisor looks at me and says: Jesse says that you asked him ... to SUCK YOUR BREAST!"

I think I am going to faint. This could not be happening to me. I have to get out where Christine will be waiting, because I have to tell her this story NOW. If I wait until the afternoon, until after the procedure, not even she will believe me, they all will think it's a hallucination after the anesthetic. But I don't think they will let me go back out. I am now the prisoner of the Hospital I am sure!

Miss Rings is relentless. "What do you think Doctor?" Terrible, I mumble; luckily she does not know what the terrible refers to. "You are telling me!!!" The voice drops still an octave, throatily she adds, "THE- MOST -TERRIBLE experience of my life! But what is that, Doctor? is that an illness? A psychiatric illness? I know that somebody said that happens to adolescents, it is like they seem normal on the outside, but they invent things, is it like schizophrenia Doctor?" It could be, I say, and I look down, and I know I must look heartbroken but on the way down my eyes have rested on the huge, huge boobs and I feel like retching, right over her desk, and like screaming I don't want to be left in this place! A hospital is a CRAZY place full of crazy people who don't even look normal!! CHRISTINE, I feel like screaming, take me home, take me home! Please! Jimmy - my thoughts fly to Palm Springs. HOW COULD YOU

LEAVE ME ALONE IN THESE CIRCUMSTANCES, WHEN I AM GOING INTO YOUR CRAZY HOSPITAL FOR A SAVAGE PROCEDURE, A NEEDLE LOCALIZATION BIOPSY?

Only once we had scheduled it, it had occurred to me to ask. I called Dr. Petersen's office and spoke to his nurse. They use a local anesthetic, right? I am sure Mrs. Coleman, but I'll ask. Two hours later and I get a call from Petersen the Great Man himself. Marianne, I thought you understood, the biopsy of course is under sedation but the needle localization… it is not really done with anesthesia… I am trembling. This is not your wild idea of a joke, is it? No, no, I am quite serious, if they used a local anesthetic, it would make the visualization more difficult. You see, they use the recent mammogram as a guide and the radiologist places the needle so as to come as close as possible to the lesion, then he confirms it with another mammogram, that way it makes it possible for me to just go straight for the lesion and remove a minimum amount of tissue… I raise my voice, feeling on the edge of madness, because the picture is unbearably clear… YES I ALREADY KNOW THAT! You already explained it, only you never told me it was done without anesthesia, JIM NEVER TOLD ME! Oh, it is not a painful thing, *really*, it is uncomfortable perhaps… At that point in the conversation my mind had become quite lucid, so I had another revelation. "What does he do with the needle then?" Petersen sounds surprised, as he asks, What do you mean? There is a long silence. The answer is obvious. I realize how stupid I will sound if I ask again, but the picture is so torturing that I must ask: What does he do...? I guess he leaves the needle in, right?

Another pause, Petersen must have thought: poor Jim, so bright a man, what a burden, she is retarded. However, he says slowly, "He leaves it in, yes, that's what will guide me, the point of the needle should be very near the calcification, of course I take the needle off when I have found the lesion and taken it out." A sort of gasp, laugh, sob, comes out of me. Ah, you don't leave it in for good? That's nice... I'm sorry, I'm sorry. So, from the radiologist to you, to the operating room, I go... with the needle sticking out?

He is patient, incredibly patient. You'll have the robe on. You'll probably be on a wheelchair, you know, hospital regulations... Enough, enough, I want to scream! No more explanations! You mean they will allow me a robe? They will not send me walking through the hospital corridors, totally naked, with a needle sticking out of my breast? Is it Andrea del Sarto's Saint Sebastian with the arrows, or Saint Agatha with the torn nipples that I remember in a panic?

Oblivious, Miss Rings sighs. "Oh Doctor, you sound so NICE, so lovely, I would like to have your card. Maybe I can call you about what happened with Jesse...."

"I will call the floor for someone to take you now… Here, this for your wrist…That IS a lovely sweater, indeed…"

Sure enough, everything goes as programmed, the radiologist is a saint, he introduces himself and then carefully explains everything again. He sticks me only twice, he says, "You are a very good patient," and he also seems to mean it when he says, as he is trying, I know how uncomfortable it is, you are really very brave.

The thing is right against my chest, and I realize that if it was… out there… more in the breast itself… it would be worse. While this is going on, I can hardly think about the horror of the admission, but I find myself thinking that if they take my breast at least mine are small, it would be worse for Miss Multi-stone-rings with the foster children, she must be a size D cup, extra-large.

Indeed, there is a wheelchair but then they let me get on the table by myself. The anesthesiologist arrives, we chat a little, when he says to start to count I actually try to think of my Jim's wonderful face, and of the phone call two days ago, when I pleaded, Jim I am serious, you understand, you are not even here, we are three hours apart in time at this moment, don't you see, and thousands of miles apart, and you have to tell me, what will you feel if they take off my breast? I could hear his grin: Actually, baby, I'll like you more, much more… I am a bit afraid of confessing this, you know, I never told you because you would have insisted that I need analysis, but my dream as a kid was to make it with an Amazon…Don't tell your friends the shrinks though, they'll know for sure I'm a pervert…

I was not totally mollified though, and I demanded, This is not a time to joke! Then another pause, just imperceptible, just enough for him to really take my anxiety in, and just like over twenty years ago he still knew to say the right things. Marianne, if you only have one breast I will have to love it and kiss it and reassure that lonely little breast so much more then!

I must be grinning to myself, now, remembering, and obediently I count as I go under…

Later, Christine will take me home…

Still later, the results. Still later, now, I look at myself in the mirror with both my small boobs that (so far!) I've managed to keep, despite my family history. And I remember some things and not others. I feel badly that I do not remember Dr. Wonderful Radiologist's name. I just keep hearing his voice saying, "You are very brave." My Jim instead said, you see, I told you everything would be all right.

I decided not to go to my mother -in law's funeral. Ronnie has met somebody else!

Miss Rings never called for a consultation. And I probably should not have seen her.

I was eight years old back then, when my father said, holding my mother's diamond ring, Marianne, one day this will be for you. I was about six when it all had started. If I remember right, she didn't have any kind of biopsy, they didn't do it that way then. They just took off the breast. Too late in her case. My aunts said to me once that they believed she must have known the tumor was there for some time but she was afraid of the surgery, afraid of losing her breast.

Jim didn't want me to wear a diamond ring that, at the time, he could not afford, so, after a while, I stopped wearing it.

But it was months after the biopsy that my youngest daughter had an assignment on Elizabeth Bishop. And then I remembered that poem, about the huge breasts in National Geographic. Hanging, I think she called them. She was a seven-year-old going to the doctor with her aunt with the Spanish name. How could I have forgotten it? I wish I could find it now. In my childhood, I too had seen issues of National Geographic. For her, I remember, it was 1918. "In the waiting room", that was the name of the poem. For me it must have been 1944. Another war was going on. My mother was already gone from my life, and I had believed what they told me about Heaven. And I also believed when they had said, so vaguely, "Your mamma was very ill, very weak." Nothing, absolutely nothing about breasts. But I must have heard the rumbles, I must have seen my aunts fearfully touching their breasts, their small and chaste breasts, and, somehow, on that day in 1944, I had been looking at magazines, and the black beautiful breasts jumped at me from the pages of National Geographic. I closed my eyes in horror. It all happened at once. I knew. I knew that small white breasts were dangerous agents of death. Those black gigantic breasts below the beads on the neck, below the smiles full of shiny beautiful white teeth would never cause anybody to die. I opened my eyes again. I wanted to cry but my father was across the room. I wanted to cry and did not know why. I wanted to cry but only into beautiful black breasts that would shelter me from the world.

THE CRYSTAL ROOM

They were lingering over breakfast like they did so many weekends, when she would look so much like her mother, a tiny version of that never-forgotten face, the colors more subtle, being that she also had some of his mother in her, the gold shining through the copper in her hair, the sea of green leaves in the incredible pools of her eyes reflecting other hues, grays and blues, from his own family. He found her so beautiful that it hurt his heart at times, when he thought, how can I love her so much and also accept she has to grow away from me? She is beginning to change now, I see the small points she tries to hide under her huge, too huge T-shirts. She hugs me at a distance, her arms around my neck, balancing herself almost "on point," careful that our chests don't touch. How will she face boys now, and then men, will I know the words that will carry her through? Will she keep me away, will she lean on me?

There were moments in which despite the way things had turned out, despite that he felt grateful for what he had now in his life, he felt bitter and full of sorrow for her, for his lovely only daughter, orphaned so early, left with a scar so huge that nothing could really heal her, he believed, nothing would ever be the same for her. Here she was, pensive, melancholy, her lips a bit parted as she read the letter, a letter she had picked up from the mailbox a short while ago, inexplicably, since the mailman had not come by yet, not making any effort to hide what she was doing, yet clearly involved in something of her own. She had not uttered a word about it. He had watched her run out, her robe flying behind her, her longish pajama-clad legs running the distance in seconds, and he had watched as she opened the mailbox, seemingly with an expression of certainty something would be there. Yet a strange shadow had fallen over her face as she looked inside. She had taken the envelope out and studied it, seeming unaware of him although she knew his weekend routine, she knew he might be watching her through the kitchen window as he got their breakfast ready.

She had looked at the envelope front and back, stood there quietly, then quite deliberately put the envelope into her robe pocket. Was he supposed not to notice? Not to ask?

Then they had breakfast on the porch, chatting about his and her week. This time much of their chatter was about Meryl and what the two "girls" had done, and the coming wedding. She told him—although she must know that he already knew—that she had gone with Meryl to another fitting of her dress, the big exciting issue being that she, Sheila, could peek at Meryl's wedding gown and he couldn't. "You know Daddy, you can't see it until the last minute, at the church, when she comes in, not before!" She sounded so serious about this notion and therefore so childish that he had to try not to smile. Almost in passing she had said, I love Meryl Daddy, she's so much fun!

Now here she was reading her letter while he glanced at the early sections of the Sunday paper. She looked worried, yet not unhappy, totally absorbed.

He thought hard before he broke the silence. This may be a pretext for me to have the chat I have been meaning to have, he thought.

"You got a letter" he said matter-of-factly.

"Yes," was the eager yet laconic answer.

"May I ask from whom? "

A boy," was the not too surprising answer. Now the silence weighed on him more heavily than before.

"Someone you like?"

"No, no, not really, but I mean, he is nice… I don't *not* like him, but I don't really like him. It's hard to explain."

He smiled openly now, relieved. Well, he thought, the moment has come. The moment for what, he wondered.

"Sheila," he started "You know, you're growing up so fast, I wonder, do you have things you want to ask?"

"About what?" was the genuinely innocent answer.

"You know, about boys, things like that."

"No Daddy, not yet."

He smiled again. However, he pressed on. "No, I mean, I'm sure you're not in love with someone yet, or anything like that, but you will be, and in the meantime, there are things that girls your age start to feel, questions you may have, I mean."

"No Daddy." She started to shake her head. Almost immediately a tension invaded her face. It was so visible that his heart raced as he saw her stumble, insisting "No, no", without conviction now.

"Are you sure?"

"Yes, I'm sure," she said much more softly. They both paused, looking into each other's eyes.

"There may be things you are puzzled by." She was silent. "No?" She half nodded, giving in, looking faintly defeated yet clearly expecting him to find a way to help her say more.

He carefully considered his words. "I know grandma may seem too old, how about Meryl?" He was shocked by her response. She reddened so dramatically he was heartsick, she was now truly breathless. "No, no!" she said, unmistakably horrified now.

My God, what could it be, he wondered. She definitely feels so bad about talking about this, whatever it is—a minute ago she loved Meryl, but this cannot be shared with her. She is MY daughter, after all, I have to be available to her.

He wanted to plunge in, insist, TELL ME! but he knew that would frighten her.

Troubled yet determined. he considered his options.

Again a long silence. She has done something, what? She says she is not ready for boys yet, was she lying? Has she done something without knowing what she was doing? Or someone did something to her? She's afraid?

"You know, there's nothing that I wouldn't accept, nothing that you should be afraid of"

She looked at him with searching eyes, eyes that were shouting, Can I trust you Daddy, can I?

Somehow, he would remember later, for many years to come, that he had stumbled upon the magic words almost by accident.

"There are things people do without meaning to, and when you care about somebody all you care about is that they feel at peace, so it does not matter if they've done something or not, if they meant to or not. I feel that way about you."

She started, slowly. "You know Daddy, when you used to come into my room late at night, to kiss me good night, when I was little?"

When she was little! He did not know whether to laugh or cry. Only a few months earlier, she had said, "Daddy, I don't think you should come into my room late at night. I might be asleep, and it could wake me up, and I have to wake up so early for swimming practice."

He had read between the lines, and knew this pronouncement signaled some rite of passage in her mind. He could not connect it clearly with Meryl's presence in their life. Meryl had gradually become more available to her, and they had started to talk openly about their wedding plans after she had asked: "Daddy, are you going to get married, because it IS all right with me, you know." Did she feel he had no right to come into her bedroom at night after that? Or had she sensed the seriousness of his commitment to Meryl and resented it in some way?

He nodded, "Of course I remember."

"Well, I had a dream." His heart leaped with relief, but immediate apprehension followed, was she going to say something he could not handle?

"In the dream I was in bed, just as always, I mean always then, and you were coming in to kiss me good night like you used to, and you came over, and ...you leaned over like you always did, and instead, then, you pulled the covers" —she made the gesture, violently, as if yanking her arm "and I was naked! And then I woke up."

He was certain that until the day he died, he would remember this moment. It would change somewhat over the years, it would bring tears or a smile or both, but the enduring image in his mind was that as he had run about the house opening familiar doors, one had led to a totally new and magical place. A crystal room. A crystal room where tender flowers grew, where rose petals rained, extremely slowly, the way snowflakes fall in those small glass ornaments, winter gardens that you turn upside down… A crystal room so delicate and beautiful that, standing at the threshold, he dared not go in, because not only might he break something in his clumsiness, but because his presence was a sheer miracle and he should only gratefully glance inside for a brief moment. He had been allowed to see into the precious garden, something, he knew, that most fathers didn't ever glimpse.

He moved slowly, full of reverence and love.

"Oh, you know, when kids grow up, the first time, well, as they start having feelings about their bodies, feel new things happening—their feelings *naturally involve the people they've grown up with…*"

He could see her tension fade, the gratitude in her eyes. Again the glow under her skin. She looked more vulnerable, in a way, than she had ever looked before, closer to him in that vulnerability, and yet on her path, a path that would inevitably lead her away. ""Oh," she sighed with relief.

Then she turned to the letter still in her hand. "Daddy, do you think I have to like this boy?"

"No sweetie." He smiled openly now. "But trust me you will like some boy. When the time comes."

Sometimes, as he grew older, he imagined himself dying, Sheila married, with children of her own, at his bedside, and only then, he would say to himself, would he give her back her gift, telling her that because of it, he knew he had done something right in his life, for her to have opened this exquisite space for him, ever so briefly, ever so magically, ever so lovingly. And yet, in all the changes of scene he imagined, this invisible path of light would join her to him, through the glittering and the velvet rose petal rain, and her lovely adolescent face reflecting on the crystal.

HOSPITAL VISIT

When we arrive he is alone in the room; it is a double room, but the other bed is empty. I can't believe the way he looks, although when Renata last saw him she told me, He's lost a lot of weight. That was more than five months ago. We haven't seen him in over five months, except me, that time at MOMA, and every day of those five months we waited for his phone call.

Renata was supposed to be a witness to the signing of his will. That was discussed several hospitalizations ago, maybe a year back. We arranged a date. The night before, however, Jack called and said, Mario says it won't be necessary for Renata to come to the hospital tomorrow. He's made other arrangements. He sounded strained on the phone, and I asked, Are you there with him? Yes, Jack said. Can I talk to him? No, Jack said, he says he is very tired.

But of course, gradually we realized something else was going on, something was wrong. As usual, as we had done for the past couple of years, we called and left messages on his answering machine: Mario if you don't feel like talking have Jack give us a call, let us know what's going on. It became routine not to hear anything for a few days, rarely, for as long as a couple of weeks. Usually not Jack but Mario himself would call after a few days. "I am O.K. ragazzi, not to worry, I'll call you soon." Jack had sometimes been the one to make the call: when Mario got pneumonia, because he could hardly breathe, or when the first Kaposi was diagnosed, because Mario was devastated, or when they both thought Mario had encephalitis and Jack himself was terrified. Jack would usually say the same thing. "Guys, Mario wanted me to call you, he's at the hospital again, he doesn't want visitors yet, but I'll call back in a few days, when he's ready to see you." Indeed, after a few days the phone would ring and one of us would go. More often Renata.

She had been there the first day of the first hospitalization, almost two years ago. It had been Jack who'd called that time too, but he had called from the hospital room, and Renata had been home early from work and insisted on speaking to Mario right then and there. When she got the story she realized Jack had not been home in more than two days, because they had been kept in the Emergency Room at Roosevelt Hospital for two days waiting for a bed. Then she said, I'm coming so Jack can go home and at least change and rest for a while. No argument, she'd said, I am coming.

Jack lives in New Jersey; they would have moved in together, into Mario's apartment in the city-—they have been together for the last few years—but Mario's sister was always supposed to visit from Italy, and it would have been uncomfortable for everybody. Mario's sister hasn't come, though. She probably wants to come when there is no more to do than dismantle the apartment and make sure she gets Mario's art collection. We knew that's what the will was about: to protect whatever could be protected for Jack.

So after the cancelled witnessing date, days went by without a phone call. And then weeks. We left messages. Nothing. We called the New Jersey number but Jack was never there and Jack has never owned an answering machine. Worried, Renata left a note at Mario's apartment.

No answer to the note, then Renata left a desperate phone message; finally Mario did answer. I don't want to have anything to do with you, he said. Renata was disbelieving. "What happened?"

"You know perfectly well what happened! You could not leave work to come and be a witness for my will?"

"Mario, you're wrong"—she wanted to say, "You're crazy," but the word seemed to her too close to the truth at that moment. "There must have been a misunderstanding, I made the arrangements when you first called, remember? I only asked if the will could be signed in the evening, so I wouldn't have to ask for the time off at work, but when you said no, I made all the arrangements" —

He interrupted, screaming on the phone: "And your husband! He could not even come to see me?"

"But you said not to come," Renata pleaded. "Jack also said not to come, Jack wouldn't even put you on the phone."

He yelled at Renata again. She tried to reason with him, but it was useless. Then I called him, three times, until, finally, he called me back. He said the same to me.

With me he didn't yell, he simply said, I am not interested in you or her. It is over. Please don't call back.

Over! Renata and I held each other and wondered; does he have toxoplasmosis? It seems to have affected his brain! Oh, it will be terrible, the only end he said he could not face.

Twenty-five years of friendship, to end like this? we asked each other. It can't be happening, we said. Then Renata murmured, What can't be happening is the disease, yet it is happening! If I can't accept it, how can he? He'd rather fight with us, she said wisely, than face the truth with us.

From time to time we would call anyway, we decided. We would continue to leave messages. So we did. Then a friend from Italy came into town and I took him to the Museum of Modern Art, and there, in the Members' Dining Room, there, to my amazement, were Mario and Jack. Mario looked almost normal, he had some color, he had obviously regained some weight. It seemed unnatural not to go over to them, so I did. Jack was warm and seemed to want to talk, but Mario was distant and polite.

That night when I told Renata, she wanted to know every detail. She asked, "What did you say, what did he say, what happened, how did he look? Tell me everything. Did you confront him?" Confront him! What could I say?

Did you hug him? she asked. Hug him! "Don't you understand he was distant!" I would have hugged him, she said, I would have hugged him. It only makes it worse for him that we go along with this craziness.

What do you mean? I asked her, disturbed, knowing in some obscure way that she was right. She had always been right about him. Mario might be crazy, but he still loves us, she said. She did not have any doubts. And as usual with her intuition, or because she knows him so well, or because in some ways she is closer to him than I am, as usual—I hate to think it, but as usual—she was right.

So, we are here now after the five months of confusion and distress because last night Jack called and said, Renata, you and Marcello can come now. Mario is ready to see you guys. The doctor said he should see all his friends now.

Renata had hung up. She couldn't speak at first and started sobbing. For the first time in the last few years, ever since we knew—although I know by now that we did not find out at the same time—for the first time at least since I knew, and perhaps even since she knew, she cried. Sobs, desperate sobs that shook her entire little body, so that at first, I was sure that Mario had died. She shook her head no, but couldn't speak, she just sobbed. When I could understand something, when she could say something, I heard her say, "We were such idiots"—"We are criminals"—"We are crazy"—"We are the crazy ones, not him."

"How could we not see him all these months?" she asked over and over again. It was useless to say that it was he who had not wanted to see us, to remind her that he had acted crazy, that he'd seemed to have this conviction that we had abandoned him, that he had actually said our twenty-five-year old friendship was over. Renata kept sobbing: we should have read between the lines, we should have been there all along. There is so little time left now.

Twenty-five years. It is almost twenty-five years since I met him at Rinascita, on Via delle Botteghe Oscure. The Communist bookstore—many young and some not-so-young people browsing over radical literature. We reached for a book of poetry by Nazim Hikmet at the same time, our hands almost touched. I did not know there existed other human beings on this earth who knew about Nazim Hikmet except Renata and I. She and I had just moved in together in this wonderful little place in the Trastevere and we felt the entire world was an ignorant desert and we could prevent our own and each other's suicide only by the miracle of having found each other.

Mario was a strikingly handsome young man, and his manners were those of a Milanese aristocrat, which is exactly what he was. He said, I guess there must be another copy. We asked the store manager. No, last copy of the only Italian translation of Nazim Hikmet's poetry, of the poems the Turkish writer had written in prison. Twenty years in prison. While the bookstore guy tried to find a second copy Mario and I started talking. Vaguely, but quite disturbingly, I felt I could have fallen in love with him, had I been able to cross that barrier even in my mind. I was almost certain of where he was coming from, so I quickly spoke about Renata and how we had just moved in together. He smiled, a smile that I would come to know so well, a smile of someone who knows too much, more than he cares to know, anyway. He had already—I think—asked me to go for a drink. We could share the only copy of the Nazim Hikmet book, he said. Where had I learned about Nazim Hikmet? he had asked. At the university, in Milano, I had said. In Milano! He had thrown back that beautiful head of his and laughed. Renata would say years later, Mario's laughter is like the music of the Roman streets—it makes you feel you are home.

So what are you doing in Rome if you go to the University of Milano? he asked. We just graduated, I answered, we're here to try to work. What is your field? I have a degree in Philology

I said, I'm interested in the relationship between memory and language in bilingual people. I'm interested mostly I suppose because I am bilingual, my mother is American, I added. He had laughed again. American? He laughed that wonderful laugh. He said "American?" but in English, with a perfect American accent. Really? He went on asking questions—And Renata does what? She does graphic design now, I answered, but her degree is in art.

In art, indeed! He smiled.

Timidly I asked, beginning to enter his seemingly fascinating world, And you? I am an architect he answered, but I'm leaving Italy, he went on, Italy is full of architects, full of idiots, full of paparazzi. I am going to the States. I have an offer to teach at Cornell.

And so it began. That night I brought him home so that we could work out an arrangement about the Nazim Hikmet book, which he had insisted I buy. Certainly, I also wanted him to meet Renata, perhaps so that she would protect me from my confused feelings about him.

Renata was very reserved, as she always is with strangers. She invited him to stay for dinner and he said no, let's go out. He eyed our little place and said, It will be my treat. I have made new friends from Rome who went to the University of Milano, let's celebrate.

We discovered that we had all taken the same philosophy and literature courses. Mario loved my love of languages and words and poetry; he claimed that if he wasn't an architect, he would be a writer. We had all taken a course on de Saussure, we all had been in the psychology course taught by Cesare Musati. We hadn't been in the courses at the same time, though, Renata was sure. She said later, He is not the kind of man one would forget. I certainly would not have forgotten him, she said provocatively.

She would not really provoke me years later, talking about him, because by then we knew about him without any doubt. And yet I knew that she shared her soul with him in ways I was and still am not sure she shares it with me. Many times in the last couple of years she has said, sadly: I will miss him so much, my life will never be the same without him. I will never be the same.

When she and I had that horrible fight in our old apartment near Columbus Circle, on Christmas Day—was it about twelve years ago?—I was so furious I wanted to kill her. She said if you go on like this I'm leaving. I screamed "Leave, leave, I don't ever want to see you again, drop dead!" I dragged her to the door. She had no coat on, no money, no keys, I pushed her out and locked the door behind her. I went back to the bedroom to watch TV, I had drunk a lot and fell asleep. When I woke up it was well past midnight. Immediately I remembered the fight.

I went to the door and opened it, but Renata wasn't there. In the morning when we both had to go to work, she showed up. The Super must have opened the door for her. She had a heavy sweater on. We didn't speak about it for days. Actually, we didn't speak at all for days, I knew I hadn't been in a rational mood that night but I couldn't say anything to her.

Finally one evening I hugged her, possibly the only time in our life together that I was able to say to her, "I'm sorry, I'm sorry, please forgive me." Later still, in bed, I dared ask, What did you do that night? After a pause she said, I went to the Plaza Hotel. With what money? She answered tonelessly, "I told the desk clerk that I'd give him my American Express number in the morning and I gave him a blow job." It took me a while, in the long silence that followed, to realize that I would never find out the truth. I'm sorry, I said again.

I decided she could only have gone to Mario's, because she would, in her loyalty to me, not have gone to anybody who didn't love me. But I was not sure, she never said, and Mario didn't say anything either. I never asked about that night again. I thought Mario was distant for a long time after that but I was never sure. He had met Olivier, his young Parisian love of the time, and maybe that's the reason he seemed distant.

I know that from the beginning we loved him in different ways—but profoundly, both of us. She was always freer with him. After her initial reserve of that night in Rome, she studied him for a while. Then one night we went to see Gassman with the Teatro Popolare Italiano doing Pirandello's Questa Sera se Recita a Soggeto. She had tears in her eyes when, over coffee at Mario's studio, we started to talk about the play. He leaned over and hugged her, kissed her on the cheek, and said, Ragazzina, piccola, they are not real, they are not real people, don't cry over them, there are enough tragedies in the world. She laughed through her tears, especially because she knew him well enough by then to know how little he lived by that wisdom, he who could become wildly passionate arguing about whether Emma Bovary's death was truly inevitable. His tenderness for her melted any mistrust she had harbored in her heart, and from that moment on she loved him.

Now he is alone in the room, and when we come in he smiles radiantly, his smile still wonderful in his emaciated face, and he says "Ragazzi, comme andate?" as if the five months had not passed, as if we had just run into him on Columbus Avenue as we often used to once we all came to live on the West side.

We both hug him and kiss him, we bring chairs next to the bed, both on the same side as he instructs us to do. Make yourselves comfortable, he says, yet there is something empty in his look. Where's Jack? we ask. He went to get something, he'll come back, Mario answers.

We start talking, he half-answers our questions and then wanders off, seems to forget where the sentence started.

However, he looks at me intensely and, smiling again, says, Marcello, why are you so sad? Don't look so sad!

Sad! I feel not sad but devastated! What has happened to his mind? It had taken Renata and me some time in Rome to realize that he was a fabulous architect, but we knew from the start that he was brilliant. He was so erudite and curious and passionate. He knew about art, about literature, about politics. It took a while to figure out that he had energy left to devote to a profession at which not only did he make a living but was prominent.

Another few sentences. Renata chats incessantly and he answers, begins to answer, but trails off. Again he looks at me and insists, Don't look so sad! What's the matter? What's happening? Is everything O.K.? I try to say something. Bewildered, I begin to feel that I want to cry.

I realize that Renata has turned to me and is glaring at me, sending me some silent message, then she turns to him and continues her questions and chatter. Simple subjects. simple questions. Jack said your sister is coming. When is she coming? He murmurs something. And your niece and nephew? Oh… they were in… they went to… my niece, … he trails off and his face falls. He says things that make no sense. You know my niece… The papers were in the other box, I have to find the tickets…

A year and a half ago, Mario's niece needed a recommendation for Cornell School of Architecture. She had visited New

York several times but this was the only time she would see Mario. On the surface, Mario had sounded pleased and excited, and exhaustively prepared every detail of the visit, wrote the letter of recommendation, rented a car to drive her to Ithaca himself, got tickets to Broadway shows, kept Jack hidden in New Jersey, got ultraviolet rays to make himself look as if he had a tan, asked all his friends, gay or straight, if they knew any young people she could meet. He went with her to Ithaca, she had her interviews, went to one Broadway show with him, said she had other tickets with people she knew from the Italian Embassy, and then stayed with a friend on the East side because she felt it was "more convenient."

Mario informed us of all this as it took place. Renata and I had planned to invite them together for dinner, but the niece had other plans and that night Mario came alone. He didn't complain, didn't say anything against niece or sister, just informed us of these developments, told us he loved the food, played with our children before we put them to bed, and after dinner reminisced with us as usual about the old days. We talked about current plays, books. It was also that evening when we realized that no one in his family except his sister knew about his HIV status. He said matter-of-factly, she feels she can't cope with it, that's why it would be hard for her to come. She will come if I really need her to.

Now he looks lost. The word" tickets" hangs in the air, incongruous. Renata says brightly, We have tickets to see Peter Brook at BAM. He picks that up, his face changes for a moment, brighter, Oh, Peter Brook is wonderful. Is he doing…? He strains to find the rest of the sentence but in his silence she picks up again, Yes! she exclaims brightly. Remember his Carmen at the Vivian Beaumont, nothing quite like it, yes Mario? Remember how mean the critics were? Again, he seems to follow her. Oh, the *American* critics! What do they know… My niece… He seems to remember the earlier question, his face so sad. He looks at me again. Renata jumps in. Young people today are so frivolous! Don't you think so Mario? This seems to do it, he responds vivaciously, You're telling me! They don't seem to even read; they are into such shallow empty things! The words flow for a while; she uses simple sentences, picks up phrases from him that she manages to regurgitate in some way, a way that only she knows, feeding him back something that his brain can absorb for a brief moment.

My own brain is on a single note: Why did he have to be gay? Why couldn't he be straight? His whole life would have been different. He would be healthy, he would live, we would not be visiting him at this grotesque floor in Roosevelt Hospital. He would be healthy now. His luminous mind is gone, and it didn't have to happen.

He looks at me again. I realize that Renata's efforts to engage him are so insistent because of me. I am full of admiration and horror at what she is doing. He says again, Marcello, don't be so sad!

Suddenly, his face changes as he listens to something internal, then a seemingly interminable moment, then we hear the uncontrolled bowels sounds, so does he, we soon smell the pungent smell, we realize what has happened even before he says: "Oh, …Mi dispiacce tanto, ragazzini, perdonatemi…" He looks around to ring for the nurse, but Renata jumps up, I'll get somebody, she says. She looks at me, either afraid of leaving me alone with Mario or wanting herself to be left alone with him. I am paralyzed. So she says quite forcefully, Stay here a minute, and disappears. I can hear her yelling outside, Nurse! She comes back in an instant. The nurse is coming, she announces. Mario keeps apologizing, I am sorry, *kids*…Ragazzi, I am sorry…

Indeed the nurse, a tall male nurse with eye make-up and platform sandals appears and takes in the situation, although Renata is already giving instructions. He needs to be changed, she is saying, We'll wait outside.

We stand outside, she blasts me: Why are you looking at him like that? Can't you make an effort? I shake my head, "No, I can't stop thinking that he could have lived so differently if he hadn't been gay. I can't get that out of my mind." Renata's anger softens immediately as she looks at me in disbelief. Then she says, "You've lost it, poor sweetheart, you have lost it. It's really gotten to you; you sound like his father would sound if he knew."

Precisely! I agree with her, because I have also been thinking of Mario's aristocratic father, living in retirement in Rapallo in great splendor, wanting to know only of his son's triumphs, the move to New York, the lecturing at a great American university, the wealthy clients that supported his son's and his own lifestyle, the designs that made it to the Museum of Modern Art, the magazine covers, the awards, never wanting to know about his son's real life, never wanting to travel to New York, never acknowledging any of the loneliness or pain.

"I know," I say to Renata, "I know, but I can't help it. Now he's going to die, and he shouldn't have to die, he could have been straight and he wouldn't die." She holds me, she puts her arms around my waist and her head on my chest and mumbles, "You are an idiot my poor love, you're a little crazy today, I know, you're saying stupid things. Just please try not to seem so sad, try to think of how he sees you."

I don't understand you, I say, Aren't you sad? How can you talk like that, as if he made sense? She gets angry at me again. What's so difficult? She makes an effort to lower her voice, then decides to pull me away from the door to his room. She takes

my arm and shakes it: Just follow some of the words, follow…
the music. You studied philology, didn't you? So you know
about words don't you? So INVENT something! That way he
won't realize that he doesn't make sense. I'm afraid he'll be
devastated if he realizes!

I am amazed at her: You think he doesn't? She answers, I
don't know, but I don't want to make it worse for him. He's
always so …considerate, even in his confusion he apologized
to us for what just happened, it really breaks me up that he's
not so out of it that he didn't realize it! And he was concerned
for us—for us! He knew what was happening and he felt bad
for us, and he called us "Kids" like he always did. She has tears
in her eyes, shakes her head. "I don't want him to see I've been
crying. And you are an idiot with your ideas about gayness
and straightness!"

Maybe it's the mother in her, I think. That's what she was
doing earlier, like a mother bird with her fledglings, feeding
him little pieces of predigested thought.

The lines of an old forgotten poem stir up in my mind…

> I am sitting like an invalid
> on the deserted dunes of my desire for you
> The fledglings you seeded onto my heart
> are trembling…
> Sometimes,

I would give them back their freedom
since they clamor to return to you…

I stop myself, wondering what is going on under my anger. I feel my face must be reddening. Then I see that Renata is looking at me, and she asks, "What's going on? Are you blushing? You are a total idiot my love, such an idiot, you are …quaint, in a way. You inject some strange perverse humor into this gloom" she adds. "I might have counted on your homophobia to introduce a different note into all this."

I know she is right. I should have been able to figure out his homosexuality with certainty very early on but I didn't want to know. When we still lived in Italy, each time I saw him with a woman I'd feel some hope. Some crazy hope. In part, I realize, to protect myself from my own feelings. Sometimes I'd say to Renata, Do you think maybe this one will work out? She would look at me the way she looks at me tonight, as if I were a being from a strange planet.

I must make a real effort now and not let him see my sadness. But shouldn't I reveal to him some of what I feel? Is it better to pretend? Is what Renata is doing honest? In some part of my mind I know I am furious, I scream at him, Why did you have to be gay?

The first time I came to see him during his first hospitalization, the bed next to his was occupied. A cadaveric figure babbling and moaning and, from time to time, howling. Renata had told me to be prepared. I'd spoken with Mario on the phone before coming to see him, and I had heard the howling in the background. Yet I could not possibly have been prepared. Mario was fully conscious, coherent, rational, he was quite scared about himself, but regarding the vestige of a human being who was lying in a fetal position, letting out those animal sounds, he had only a terse comment: I hope I can get a private room soon. I started to think it then: Is he going to end like this creature? Why did he have to be gay? I tried to push these thoughts away. That first visit Jack had arrived with flowers, and as he'd put them in a vase, I thought, It's exactly like a woman, it's so absurd. Back home I tried to say something about this to Renata, but she said some of the things she is saying now—My love, Marcello dearest. As usual, you are a little old fashioned, a little homophobic, a little boy, a lost boy from *un piccolo paese.* I'm a bit embarrassed about you, but thank God, you are not really mean.

The nurse comes out and says, You can go back in.

So here we are again. He seems much better and may have forgotten the humiliation of a few minutes ago. Or maybe he's past humiliation.

Renata goes on with her choreography of sentences that he can more or less follow, picking up his loose words and building something about them. I try to do the same.

In part it is her doing this so masterfully that distracts me. I know she will never leave me, but when I look at what she does for him, at the way they connect, I know that he's filled something for her that I will never fill. And maybe she's never been unfaithful to me because of him, because of the way she feels about him.

We go on with our visit, me trying to follow Renata's cues. Finally, we see Mario is very tired, we ask if we should leave. Yes please, ragazzi, he says, Come back tomorrow.

We hug, we say, I love you. When Renata holds him, she clings to him a moment too long. She turns to me, and I see her eyes are filled with tears again.

Outside we run into Jack coming out of the elevator with packages. I'm glad you had time alone with him, Jack says. We know he is totally sincere about it. He truly adores Mario, and he has always accepted us.

We walk back home slowly, in the early evening full of spring perfumes. We get two blocks from home and Renata looks towards the river and says, Let's not go home yet, I don't want the children to see that I cried, let's sit in the park. We find a bench and we sit. In that polluted sky the incendiary red of the sun going down over New Jersey is too beautiful, too painfully beautiful for words. In our shared silent grief we sit holding hands.

I am overwhelmed by fragments of memory. I ask Renata, The night he told me about the H.I.V., I came home and I told you and you said you knew, how did you know? How long did you know?

He told me, she answered. He told me a long time ago. You were quite worried about getting your tenure at the time, remember? He said you had enough on your mind. I promised him I wouldn't tell you until he was ready to share it with you.

I think to myself that perhaps he was not just protecting me, perhaps he didn't want me to know for his own sake. He did not want to acknowledge it to me, as a man. My thoughts go in opposite directions, Did he ever think of our hands almost touching years ago at the bookstore? Did he think as I do that his life could have been very different?

I say to Renata, Thank God for Jack, because homosexuality is a monstrosity. It's terrible anyway, the relationships are a monstrosity, and these days homosexuality is also lethal.

Renata says softly, Oh, I see. Marriage is not a monstrosity? True, it is generally not lethal. She sighs. Men are strange animals. Life is much harder for you men, I guess, she adds.

Her words are suspended between us. I am not as angry as I sounded, she adds, then goes on, We'll talk some other time.

The setting sun and the river soothe me after the sights of the hospital, but the respite is brief. I find myself thinking, Will he ever see this river again, will he come out of the hospital this time?

Renata interrupts my thoughts. We'll have to take turns, it's going to get worse, we won't be able to go every day. Every day! Indeed, we couldn't stand it every day! She is thinking like a sister or a mother. Like a sister or a mother who loves and cares, as his real sister should have cared.

I get angry at Mario again. He's going to die, I tell her, without children—what kind of life did he have? Why did he ruin his life? He could have left children in this world.

Renata has answers, passionate answers: He leaves beauty! He leaves beauty behind! All the beautiful things he created and the beautiful buildings! And he lives in us and in other people who loved him and whom he loved! And he himself was, is, beautiful, his mind and his heart were, are, still beautiful! I'm sorry the children have not known him better, will not really have known him, I'm sorry we can't bring them to the hospital!

It's her turn to be a little crazy, I think, and I hold her. Let's go home, she says. I agree, Yes, we'll talk tomorrow.

We both know that perhaps we'll never talk, we know that what lies ahead is just more terrible hospital visits, just that, until the end, and perhaps past that end we won't really talk, either, about how we each feel different feelings about him. Perhaps the hospital visits will consume our differences, or perhaps they will become worse, a vast space between us, where she'll be the sister he should have had, loyal to the end, and I...What will I be, I wonder? Will I make peace with my tormented love for him?

As we leave the park, we talk about when we'll tell the children that he is dying.

LAST RITES

He did not think he had made any sound. Was it dawn already? In the dark his wife's hand reached up from behind him, under his arm, along his chest, gently, towards his face; she gently touched his tears; then, ever so softly, as she would with a child, she turned him over towards her. Facing him now, she let her fingers wipe his cheeks, began to kiss him softly, soothingly, no pressure, no demand in her kisses, just her heart flowing out to him, unquestioningly, as usual. He let out a sob, convulsed, totally revealing now, despite himself, not because he was afraid to hurt her with his grief, but because his grief was so private, so much a part of him, he thought, that not even she should have a glimpse of it. Then gratitude and tenderness turned into habit and his body responded to her as if what guided him was passion; he searched desperately, clinging, holding on to life. The thought flashed through his mind: *this is bizarre. I make love to Muriel while my heart is breaking, exploding in pain over Giovanna.* He didn't want to push Giovanna away, even if the scene in his mind seemed … almost indecent, and anyway, even if he tried, the memory of the fragile body would burn him evermore. And in a flash he realized the more he hurt for that destroyed body, clinging to life in the hospital room only a few miles away, the more his own body, healthy, blindly determined, furious, made his demands on his wife more urgent, more necessary, more inevitable. Then sex was over, the world was the same as before, and he felt grateful, perhaps almost happy.

Yet in the center of his chest, this certainty remained, oppressing him like a torture instrument, this simple thought: Giovanna is dying, is going to die soon, any minute now. My former wife. The mother of my children. He knew any minute he may get the phone call. He had told his children- his daughter rather, but he always hoped that he could think of both of them in the same way, he had asked her, please, as soon as they know, as soon as she knows, to let him know. Shouldn't he be with his children tonight? But where, where would he, could he, be *together* with his children? In *their* home, the home that Peter had built? For the last few days and nights the children would not come and stay with him and Muriel. It wasn't only that Peter had asked them not to, he was certain of it, they themselves wanted to be *at home*. The words had always been hurtful, although he understood… or tried to understand. He often would try to counteract the effect- who was he trying to fool? - by saying "mommy's home" and " daddy's home". " *Why don't you bring your skies to daddy's home over winter vacation, dear?"* Or, quite devastatingly: *"Yes, of course you can take these toys with you, to mommy's home."* But now, now it was worse, and more, much more devastating: the question burned hm, what business did he have in his children's lives? Yes, he'd get them legally, but, horror of horrors: should he get them? His daughter was full of love for him, he could feel it all the time. She was full of love and understanding and compassion. She has compassion and love also for Peter, the thought emerged mercilessly. She was the perfect oldest child; sensitive to everybody's needs, articulate, responsible. Always doing what's right. *Just like her mother*. Why can't I let go of this sarcasm?—he thought sadly.

Just yesterday evening, as he was taking his daughter home in a cab, home to *her* home, of course—*there I go again*—home from the hospital, she had rested her head on his shoulder, crying silently, squeezing herself against him, in the same gesture, the same exact gesture! with which her mother, twenty years before, had reached out to *her* father... How young they had been then! He had felt jealous, useless, discarded, at the Cemetery -just a supposed friend, not part of the family, since his involvement with Giovanna had been kept secret, precisely because Giovanna's mother had been so sick, near death, and they feared her reaction. Giovanna's mother, the bulwark of the strict Catholic family, would not look with favor upon her daughter's involvement with a heretic, a militant socialist. So he had been peripheral, just one of many faces and certainly peripheral and useless at the funeral, when Giovanna had rested her head on her father's shoulder as her mother's coffin was lowered, and all he could feel was insane fury against that philanderer father, and the wish to seize Giovanna and carry her out of there, away, somewhere where there would be no family, no memories, no social tensions and no pretense.

So now is now, and my daughter rests her head on *my shoulder*, he thought, as her mother lies dying, and yet I am again (or should I say still?) peripheral.

Yet his daughter was always reaching out to him, even times when he didn't know what to respond, often feeling his own words were so inadequate. On the taxi, softly, she had said. "Daddy, did you know that Peter brought her a priest?" His heart stood still. *Oh?* She went on: "He told me after he had done it, I mean... I guess, do you think that mommy would have wanted it? You think she minds?" He tried to think calmly about who was it who was important now, who he should craft the answer for. Yet his mind was racing: there *he goes* again: the last irony and the last insult for Giovanna and for the children. Would Giovanna had time, no, did she have time to think, to talk to Peter about it? Would Peter claim that it was she who had asked for a priest? Already, hadn't Peter, who by himself had arranged for the specialists and for the Catholic hospital and for the specific kind of treatment and all under the cover:

"*We* discussed it already" done enough? The *we* Peter used was not quite as dreadful as the *home* the children used but it came close. Yet the Giovanna I married, he said to himself, had given up the Catholicism of her childhood, they had decided not to bring up the children as Catholic, they had together planned a life that tolerated his political activism and yet preserved some respect for her past. He had never thought though, in all truth, that she was free of that past. Such awareness had evoked his angry reproaches about their restricted sex life, it had fueled his demands that she free herself from what in his youth he called her Catholic rigidity. The awkward, hurried, hidden moments before their marriage had made him think that he would conquer her fears. And it had seemed so for a while, until their daughter was born. Then Giovanna had become a mother. No longer a wife, she didn't want to leave their baby daughter with anybody, not even her family, she didn't want to go away with him for a weekend, she was exhausted at night and rushed in the morning.

Fragments of a long-forgotten, almost buried picture began flashing in his mind, a blind picture he thought, an irrational image- and instinctively he pushed those fragments down to the darkness of the ocean where they had been submerged.

Gradually he had been overcome by resentment. Then his own father had died, suddenly, without warning. So many years later now and he still only dimly understood how the world had been turned upside down after his father's death. He had become convinced that he was forever trapped in his life, a life that highlighted Giovanna's inhibitions, provincialism, something that at times seemed to border on pettiness.

Incomprehensibly, the blind picture surfaced again, vague sensations with no image, echoes without sounds.

As he caressed Muriel's head, gently, as she rested her head on his chest, he thought with dismay: God, do I still dare think of *her* pettiness? I invoke my father's death to justify that first affair and I speak of pettiness? But maybe it was true that his father's death had given oppressive boundaries to every aspect of his life at the time. It had certainly also added an intense color of urgency. How was it then, when was it, that Andy was conceived? He tried to remember, ashamed. No wonder my son at times seems a stranger, he thought in pain, not only I abandoned him when he was less than two years old, I can't even remember if I wanted him.

Yet it wasn't totally true, was it? No, nothing ever is *totally* true, he had learned painfully, was still trying to learn. Then, he remembered. When the memory came, it was even more painful than its absence. He had not made love to Giovanna in months; he had come home from a fight, a terrible fight with his mistress of those many months, feeling anguished, so centered on himself and his agony over what to do, over the demands he felt everybody made upon him, so confused, full of resentment at having gotten himself in a mess he could only keep making worse, and suddenly Giovanna had been there, so available, so grave and reserved; if *she* was in pain she never spoke of it, she just looked at him with those deep sad eyes that he had fallen in love with many years ago. He had reached out and she had responded.

A whisper in his mind, the little bits and pieces, the small sounds and sensations (of smell, of taste?) grew…. *No, I don't want to look at this picture*, he almost screamed-

For a brief, brief moment he had thought , even now, many years later he struggled with the truth, but truth had a way of pushing through, he had thought with hope.

He had actually thought: we could be happy again, me and Giovanna and our daughter and may be more children, may be a son. Years later it is, and how many times, he wondered, he had given the same stereotyped explanation, to Giovanna herself first, and then to their friends, to both families: *our sex life was miserable, we could never have been happy, we in fact were never sexually happy.* As if such statement exonerated him (or whoever made use of it for that matter) of all the responsibilities of marriage. As if it was a truly incontrovertible, a self-evident truth to be held before all men: Is it not perhaps guaranteed by the Constitution? His law career must have been incomplete if he could not remember a special amendment or at least a Supreme Court decision: All men are created equal

AND ALSO should have a happy sex life. ALWAYS HAPPY. Ecstatic, in fact.—The whisper now seemed to turn into a shout: *"ECSTATIC!"*—He persisted however in his sarcasm. There should be no interference with a person's sex life. No parents dying, no children being born. Just like that.

Finally, mercilessly, the picture that had been pushing forward in his mind was vivid, painful, obscene given the circumstances.—Giovanna's head thrown back—*in ecstasy* - she had said blushing when he later asked what she felt-They had been so young, for a few clandestine hours, during the many months of Giovanna's mother's illness, using his cousin's apartment, and he tried to appear experienced and strong. Now the pictures of sex with Giovanna started to flow, relentlessly, reminding him painfully of her intensity, of her passion. Peter knows her that way too, he thought icily for a moment.

Ah, God, God in which- or in whom- I don't believe, why do we come into this life so ignorant, and why is what we learn usually learnt for our files and of so little use for our future? Who do I have at this moment to address in this grief? I say God, like Giovanna—if she is conscious she must be addressing God, because she does believe—but I don't have anyone to reach out to. In those days I thought I had her, Giovanna herself, she's the one I want to talk to, the mother of my children, my friend from school. How could I have loved her like that and then turned her into this other person, a nun? Did I do that? Did she in fact, in documented, uncontested, honest truth, turn herself into a nun? And now, what do I do with my life now? Do I question anything? Have I learned *anything* ? Have I not just made love to Muriel as if she belonged to me like some kind of possession? He tried to offer himself some reassurance, Muriel *knows*, she knows my grief, and she is not frightened, and I know she is precious and I want to keep her.

Muriel is not frightened, he repeated to himself. Giovanna had been so frightened, so frightened of life, and he had resented it so, even without fully knowing her fears, because he himself had been so frightened and in his world, in their world... men could not be frightened. In their world! Was there such a thing? A world of theirs, really? Did they ever *share* a world? Her -Giovanna's- world had been one in which men cheated and women suffered, that is what she had grown up with. In his own world... he knew it was possible for a marriage to be miserable without any infidelity; his own parents had silently tolerated one another. He had sworn to himself many times he would never, never be trapped in a marriage such as that of his parents. Well, he certainly had not been trapped, had he? Only *felt* it. And now, years after that marriage had ended, after he had constructed what everybody else saw as a *very good* relationship with his children and even after he had found Muriel- a gift from life he thought, living proof that sometimes we get a second chance - so now, years later he questioned it all. Could he have stayed and fought?

The question struck him as academic, useless and potentially malignant. Yet he could not shake it. Could he have stayed and FOUGHT?

In regard to Giovanna he had always seen himself as the one who fought, pushed, argued, made demands. Giovanna had always followed him. She followed him quietly, and—now a renewed wave of resentment overcame him—also silently reproachful. Her quiet suffering was a reproach. The disdain with which she refused to have an argument over anything was corrosive. Whether big or small, that was totally irrelevant, the refusal to argue was much worse than a reproach. It felt to him as the total failure to arouse her *as a person,* and that was what felt truly devastating.

Then came the major, more devastating, more potentially irreversible event of life. Andy's illness. The doctor's tight face and the words: he may not make it. Andy in the hospital. Weeks of agonizing wait… and… for Giovanna and him, the beginning of the end. He had been preparing for months for his first major civil rights case, it was a unique chance for him. Every day he would phone her, but he would be at the hospital only for a few minutes, late in the evening, whereas Giovanna practically lived there. He would insist she should come home at night and he'd explain that he had to be able to sleep so he could work the next day. She understood, she said, she just must stay at the hospital, that's all.

If there was one thing in his life he might do differently, that would be it, he thought sadly. But then, would that have made a difference? Or would something else later have pushed her forever sexually away from him, and in turn his resentment exploded?

It took him—them?—one more year, after Andy got well. All the months that preceded the separation he had tried to provoke her into some response that would seem *human*. It was useless. She had lost weight, become more ethereal than ever, more concentrated on Andy but busier than ever with their daughter too, an angelical mother, she herself would say, sounding self mocking. Sometimes, she would half joke: "If my mother could see me, I've become a real—or a really *unreal* mother."

He mumbled in response to Muriel's soft inquiry—it sounded like "Mark, will you be able to sleep? Do you want to talk?" Yes, to the first question, No, to the second. I love you, he added, truthfully. Let's sleep.

But of course, he thought, I can't sleep. I don't want to sleep. I am waiting for the phone call. Giovanna will be no more. No more chance to tell her all these things, to explain, to ask for forgiveness. All chance of that now gone, and worst of all the realization, unbearably painful, after what happened in the hospital today, that even if they had been able to speak, even if she didn't require the oxygen mask- why this death, of all manners of death?- although they had assured him and all of them that she was not in pain, her lungs were filling up they explained, seeded- what an awful ironic word- seeded with metastasis - So then, even if she had been able to speak understandable words instead of that gibberish, even if he had been able to get through to her, worst of all now, he knew she had not forgiven him.

Today he had entered her room for a moment and looked at her. Peter was there, as always. There must be some decency in the man, he had thought with barely suppressed hatred, when Peter had left him alone in the room with Giovanna. Not one word, and no idea if he would come back in a minute or an hour. But at that moment, seized with tenderness and grief, he had come close to the bed and gently taken her still lovely hand in his. And to his horror, she, who could barely babble those unintelligible sounds, (sounds which Peter claimed he understood) she had slowly, deliberately , withdrawn her hand.

That is why I can't sleep he said resignedly to himself. That is what I must face. Because it may mean something: it may be a message that I must understand. I have to face it, it may be about the children. She may not want the children, specially Andy to live with me.

The only words that she had ever said to him that had any cruelty, uttered in response to his fury when he had spat at her the story of his infidelity, and threatened to leave her , those haunting words came back to him. *"It may be better for the children, specially for Andy. I suppose I should not have expected my son to have a better father than the one I had."*

We are all prisoners of our history, he thought. Somehow this certainty she had not forgiven him, painful as it was, seemed to give a finality to the events of their life together. For a brief moment he hoped: Maybe she didn't recognize me. Maybe she thought Peter was still in the room. It would be like Giovanna to think in her dying moments that it was unseemly for her ex-husband to hold her hand in the presence of her current husband! But nothing stood the test of his knowledge of her, his knowledge of thirty years, since the days of Junior High. She was clear about right and wrong and therefore had not forgiven him. She had no doubts, no vacillation about where her conscience stood. He had been unfaithful and had deserted her. The infidelity had made him like her father, but the desertion made him worse than her father. Infidelity would not have been forgiven either, but tolerated, the way her mother had tolerated it, like the bearing of a cross, part of the tragedy expectable for many women, in so many lives. The desertion had been a criminal, monstrous unspeakable act, a final act. His personal engineering of a one -couple Holocaust. She had perhaps, long before, tried to warn him about things that remain unforgiven. There are things that cannot be forgotten, lines that cannot be crossed. She had said that once, speaking of someone else. Because, she had added, some people never recover.

It was this knowledge that she did not change that a few days ago had prompted him to bring to the Hospital a taped version of Schubert's Trio in E flat, in the small cassette player which in his mind belonged to Andy, although he knew that Andy had another one at home, at home with Peter. Timidly, in the Hospital room, his daughter was there, and of course Peter was there, he had offered it to Peter, with a stammered explanation. *"When we were in College, Giovanna used to say, if she was ever very sick and unable to speak that is what she would want to hear. Do you think... Peter, do you think it may be played softly? She may hear it, she... it would ... soothe her, perhaps?"*

Was it his imagination or the steely blue eyes became steelier? After all, he thought now, I think of this as humiliating for me, but Peter must see it as humiliating for him. If Peter had said: Yes, he knew already that was one of Giovanna's favorite pieces of music- then he would have felt calmer; if Peter had said "No, Giovanna now had different tastes"- he would have known this was the polite hateful Peter response. But, of course, Peter gave the truly expectable response. Peter mumbled, "Thank you" and then " *Of course she hears, we talk*" and then Peter put the cassette player with the Shubert cassette down, obviously and provocatively away from Giovanna, on the windowsill with lots of other useless gifts that people had brought during the first few days of the hospitalization, and still kept bringing.

Today after Giovanna had withdrawn her hand from his, his eyes had searched. Surely there it still was, on the windowsill.

One by one, the small events that shaped his remorse, his humiliation, his regret, mercilessly filed, surged again in the quiet of the night. What can I do now? he asked himself. What does *Giovanna* want me to do now? I was not even able to properly reassure my daughter, he thought sadly. When his daughter had told him about the priest he had tried: "Hopefully mommy was not conscious." His daughter had insisted: Peter said the priest gave her Last Rites. Mommy had to be conscious to confess, right? Not necessarily, he had reassured her, of course not, you can give Last Rites to someone unconscious.

It was true, after all, a priest can give absolution to a person who is unconscious. Peter, after all, must know. Peter must be terrified of her soul burning in the eternal fire. Peter could not imagine that she may have been terrified to see a priest, revolted at the idea of confession, anguished with the certainty of death. For Peter, after all, the life that she would now go into would be eternal life. How could Peter reconcile her divorce with his Catholicism? He did not know but could guess. Peter had an answer for everything. Surely Peter sees her as my victim and himself as the Avenging Angel, the rescuer, the Savior. They will be always together in Paradise. Andy had said to him: Mommy and Peter and I will be together again in Paradise. Through his burning dark eyes- Giovanna's eyes, the intensity, the quiet passion - he saw that his son too had not forgiven him. They belong together, he thought with dismay. They belong together. Maybe it is true that they will be together in some form. Whichever form it is, it is not mine. My form is tortured, full of doubt.

Even my Catholicism was tortured, the Irish version. If I were still a Catholic, I would be the Liam O'Flaherty kind, maybe the Graham Greene kind. I would commit mortal sins while suffering all the time, I would end up a suicide with all my faith in God intact but pushing me towards an act I despise. Their faith is pure and certain: Andy in his seven-year-old certainty, Peter in his fifty-year- old arrogance. And Giovanna, where does she belong? She soon will belong no more, it will be irrelevant. It may already be irrelevant that I worry about the priest. Indeed, if this God who does not exist was merciful, she never saw the priest, and, if she saw him, she may not have understood what it meant,

Peter is immoral, he thought with great lucidity. Of course! You must be immoral if you are very religious! It's inevitable. Religion demands rigidity to save the soul. Morality demands flexibility, compromise to think of the complex and ever-changing needs of the living.

There! This would be a very pernicious thought for my son, I am sure. Children need a system that is steeped in assurances and stability and a certain degree of conformity. Of these qualities I possess none.

I must try to sleep. Tomorrow, tomorrow I will talk to Muriel. Should we voluntarily allow Andy- well, both children then- to continue living with Peter? Of course his daughter would be devastated. He immediately rebelled against his own thought. And he also felt sure that Muriel would be horrified. She would fight for him. She would want his children to be with the two of them.

———◆———

Oh sweet baby Jesus of my childhood, let me be well for a few hours, I don't know how many hours I have been in this room. The mask is terrible but to be without it is worse, much worse. I must live a few more hours so I can make sure that I tell Peter what I want. Peter will know for sure anyway. He always knows. But I want him to know that the children will, should be with their father. Of course, Andy would be particularly devastated otherwise. It would be terrible otherwise. And Mark wants them and he will be good to them he always has been good to them. Even when he was not so good to me....

Oh my baby Andy how I wish you could be here. You were like a gift of magic for me. And then you were so sick my sweet baby. Mommy promised then that if you were saved, she would give up all pleasure, other than you children. Oh sweet sweet baby of mine, when you came back to life I knew life could not just be so generous and not demand something in return.

I feel so terrible, it's not the pain, the air, oh God the air! It is so terrible to get no air. I wish Peter would play Schubert, that Trio, it always makes me feel that life can be beautiful. He will, I'm sure. I think I can hear it now.

I must have slept and dreamt. A priest was here, he was floating, pushing, stepping on the air that I needed, and he whispered incomprehensibly. I know that you and Peter sent the priest Mamma, but you should have told him not to step on my air tube. You see Mamma: I know how you felt, don't be angry at me, Mamma, please don't be angry, I feel you are reaching for me Mamma. You should see my baby Andy, Mamma, he has your color Mamma, and your hair and the same nose. I know you wanted a son Mamma.

Oh God they don't seem to understand. I have to get out of here and finish lots of things. I am so scared that Mamma will find out about Mark and me. Mark is so careless, he took my hand and mamma was looking at us. Mamma is so sick. God let me breathe again, please please, let me breathe on my own. I took my hand away but, too late! Mamma must have seen.

I will call Andy, no, no, he is too little. Father then? Peter, Peter will help; he always knows what to do. He will know what to do now.

Oh sweet God, don' t … I must be very delirious, confused … I think I don't really know what goes on, what went on. Mamma is it really you? Please Mamma I know you wanted a son, you almost took him but you didn't. Don't take my Andy Mamma. I'll be with you soon Mamma. Please.

Oh please, stop this, please, I need my children Don't take the children away! Don't take the children away, Peter I know you and Mamma can take the children but it's not right. I am coming instead Mamma. Oh please sweet sweet God, Mamma, no words, no, Mamma, here I come to you Mamma, to you! Please be there. Don't take my children, here I come Mamma…

—————◆—————

The phone call came at six in the morning. As he said hello he recognized his daughter's sob. She didn't suffer, daddy, it's all over now, she said. -No, he thought, it's just starting, for me.

DOCTOR

There is a scene in a Curzio Malaparte novel in which a little girl wanders into her sleeping mother's bedroom, and silently reads the phrase tattooed over her mother's shoulder. She laboriously deciphers the foreign words. The mother, as if she perceived the daughter's presence, turns toward the girl and is startled into a horrified awakening as the child says, «Mommy, I know what *Reserwierte für Ofizieren* means, it means, *Reserved for Officers*, but, *Reserved for Officers*, what does *that* mean?" For some reason that I only dimly comprehend, the scene has come to mind many times, ever since I began to think of telling this story. Or, more precisely, of dictating this story.

There is an obvious connection between different brands or nationalities of fascism, but what else? When I was thinking of my having lied I didn't think of that scene. Neither did I think of it when I went to court to testify, nor when I made my statement to the Refugee Commission.

It is only now, when I am ready to tell the whole story, that the memory surfaced.

I wonder, who do I put in the position of the little girl unable to comprehend? Then I discard the most plausible candidates, she is not necessarily my daughter, who by now knows that *bad men took daddy away* when she was very little, and did terrible things to him. It may be a version of me, in the feminine aspects of me, in traits I have that resemble my mother's, a naive incredulousness about human cruelty that the tragedies and horrors of life have shaken but not fundamentally erased, or it might be my mother herself in the shock and horror she would have felt at this story, even more perhaps because of the other connection…how many times she must have washed and changed and cared for a mutilated body!

Perhaps, however, the little girl is another child, but a boy, Luisito, for whom perhaps this story is thought out this particular way, which is by force, different from the way I told it in court or to the Refugee Commission. A story that is told many times is of course different each time it is told to a different listener. I try to remember that to help push from my mind the image of the kind but all too simple secretary who has agreed to transcribe my dictation. Because I want to think slowly and deeply about who my real listener is and why I have I chosen this time to speak. In here I have a lot of time on my hands, (terrible choice of images, given the circumstances) and also I am in a foreign land and can reflect about the way I want things to be told.

When I testified in front of the Refugee Commission, after I told them the straight facts, simply what had happened, they asked me if there was anything I wanted to add. I felt funny, especially as they said very deferentially "Doctor"...

Now that I think of this, there is an obvious connection between my registering the respectful way in which they said the word "doctor," the central point of the story I am finally going to tell, and the Malaparte scene in which there is, like there will be in my document, a shockingly dissonant note struck between the scars of the Apocalypse and the innocence of a child.. this other one now remembered....

So, the point is, when they asked me was there anything else, I only said that I was grateful that they had given me the opportunity to testify, that I knew they would publish a report and I thought that it was going to be of value. Real value, I said. Yet I knew I was lying, because—it has taken me so long to think this through, but I know now—there is no *real* value to my having told the story, or to their publishing the Report, *unless I tell the whole story* After all, people have been tortured since the Stone Age and yes, as my mother would say if she were alive, we are a lot better off because these things get published now, but of course I know better: there were no presses in the Stone Age or for a long time afterwards, and people still do not tell whole truths.

Well, I see that it is taking me a long time to get to the point and it must be for the same reasons why I lied, both in Court and to the Refugee Commission; I think more than anything else it has to do with shame. Shame is a feeling I had not felt since childhood, but have felt many times since I was released, and though I saw a therapist for a long time and we did talk about it, we talked mostly about the shame over my hands and what it would mean to me later. I could not really think clearly about what the shame was about, since I did not tell even my therapist the whole story.

While I was dictating they came to change my dressing. I avoided looking, as I always do. They said again it looks really good. However, I try not to be too hopeful, just to remind myself that they are doing their best and I, for once in my 50 years, 25 of which have been in medicine, can do very little.

I do not have a clear picture of how many days passed before the first time they left me alone after a torture session. I eventually learned that I was tortured on and off for nineteen days and then I stayed in the hospital for two months and then was transferred to the regular prison for seven months, until the International College of Surgeons intervened and I was released. I know that the story I am finally about to tell is from the time that *I think* is the first time they left me alone, but maybe I am thinking only of the first time I was conscious for a long time.

I always had a hood on, and I was still tied to the table, and I heard the door open and some noise and the sound of water splashing in a container and then the voice, a man's voice that whispered: "Doctor, I am going to wash you." What strange perception seized my mind then, and made me plead? Because I certainly knew by then the total futility, in fact the unvarying perniciousness of pleading, begging, showing any weakness. I heard my own voice, unrecognizable, saying, "No, please don't!" At least that is what I thought my voice tried to say while in the forefront of my mind I tried to imagine what as yet unknown horror, what medieval game involving *washing* this new one was, but at the same time in the depths of my dazed utterly shocked brain I must have registered the immense *deference* in the voice, the awe in that whisper which seemed apologetic and repeated itself as if I had said nothing, "I am going to wash you, doctor." *They* had used the word doctor many times in mockery, in insult, in total contempt, in all forms of sadism, in all the variations that the romance languages permit that make a noun able to change gender, size, intentionality: doctorcito, doctorazo, and even the feminizing, castrating, doctorcita, accompanied by all the imaginable sexual uses.

The power of words can sometimes be brutal. This "Doctor" sounded as none other had sounded inside the prison, it sounded indeed as like what it turned out to be, the "Doctor" that belongs in emergency rooms and evokes nights of sleeplessness and is entangled with juvenile idealism...

So there we were: the whisper and I, and in a few moments there were more noises, and then the sound of something going in the water and water being squeezed out, and then the hands over my body, gently, deferentially, the voice saying, always in a whisper, "Sorry, it is cold, there is no hot water here," and in my brain these words dancing a totally hallucinating three-dimensional, cartoon-like picture, words hysterically laughing, shouting, making a T.V. commercial, or something else, a musical, perhaps, a la Brecht and Kurt Weil: *"In this hotel, there is a wash, but, there is no hot water here, if you want to get a wash, you must get-cold water here. First get the blood, then get the shit — then there is cold water here."* I was, of course, covered, caked, in assorted body fluids, not all of them mine, and I had gotten used to the stench until he started washing me. I was still waiting, wondering: when does the blow come, when the electric current, when the as yet unimagined new fantasy of their Inquisition minds, why the whispering, what new indescribable perversion was this that I was not prepared for? Something old and forgotten seemed now stirred in me which I had lost, thousands of hours ago, in the ancient times before the days of torture. It was this old and almost forgotten feeling that until a few days ago, a million years ago, I had possessed, the feeling induced by the whisper that reminded me: *I was indeed a Doctor.* You see at first, I'm sorry, my mind keeps jumping back to this: I had not known how to answer the Refugee Commission when they said," Please tell us your occupation." Because what should I say, I *was* a surgeon? The past tense seemed appropriate since only if you can operate are you a surgeon, but I said I *am* a doctor and that seemed all right. Yet my answer has made me think about what one *is* internally as an essence… and what one is as a condition… and what one is that reflects the way others see us, and also what one acquires and what one keeps.

So there I was, rapidly becoming a doctor again, because of the way the whisper kept saying it, and I knew that this was *not* a good state to be in. So far I had been able to emotionally survive because I had not thought of myself as myself or even as a person but as something else. It had started with the first blows and the first humiliations … I would think, " They are not human," and see myself as human, and for a while that seemed to work. The insistence that they were not *real people* seemed to make the humiliations more tolerable , it didn't work quite so well against the physical pain. Later I tried something else … I would try to build a wall right under my skin, try to remember comic books of my childhood, where I would be the hero, someone from a different planet with extraordinary powers, and there I would be, impermeable to them, their insults and their instruments. Suddenly now, there I was, terrified into remembering that indeed I was a doctor, I had patients, I had, worst of all, a wife and two little children, one of them my baby daughter, and I didn't know where they were. *They,* in here, kept saying that my family would suffer terribly, but I kept hope because I was certain that if they had seized my wife they most certainly would not have spared me seeing her here, so I had decided early on that I just could not think about her and the children; that was all part of building the wall under my skin and over my brain, so that I would not feel so totally vulnerable. To think of my wife and the children also meant the possibility of self-reproaches that would destroy me. I kept trying to remember that keeping me in the hood was a good sign... that I might survive and then so might my family.

So here was the whisper, calling me Doctor, apologizing, and the hands, gentle, and helpful ...and out of this *professional* deformity I hear myself asking " Who are you?" and to my everlasting amazement I hear the answer, whispered too but unmistakable, " I am Luisito's father, remember, the three fingers..."

I get to this point in my memory, it never varies: In a flash I think that I must be completely mad, I must have been so crazed that I invented it, it never happened, or if it happened, then it was all part of a plot that remained unclear, I never understood it, it had a different purpose, it just was supposed to work some other way and it didn't. Yet I know it happened. So there I was with Luisito's father. There may have been other Luisitos in my life or in my practice, but there was no way I could not identify *that* Luisito with the three fingers. The three fingers had been dangling then, that unbearably hot afternoon in which father, hysterical mother and hysterical four-year-old Luisito had appeared in the hospital emergency room, Luisito's hand with the badly severed fingers wrapped in a blood soaked table napkin. I was a surgery resident full of the usual conceit of all surgery residents, and I had taken over. Although I had only assisted in the surgery, I had been the one designated to deal with the parents, the one making the long stop at rounds, the one playing with Luisito later. Later still, I had become Luisito's and Luisito's family's unofficial "family doctor". They knew when I was on call, they knew my telephone extension at the hospital, they would consult me about consulting anybody else. As Luisito's fingers were saved, although they would always be deformed, I became the surgeon, the Savior, the doctor above all doctors. I'd say it had not been me, I 'd take out of my white coat pocket the money they would try to stuff into it whenever I answered their medical questions, I'd gently quarrel with them and say they needed to get a regular practicing doctor. It was all in vain. Until I left the residency, and since they lived in the neighborhood—I only vaguely knew that Luisito's father worked at an Air Force Base in some janitorial job—they would come in for every emergency, and sometimes for no emergency, just to chat or to bring a present.

I then left for two years abroad, lost all contact with them. When I came back, it was to a University appointment at a much more renowned hospital, and a rapidly developing private practice.

So here we were, how many, over twenty years later? I wanted somewhere to ask about Luisito, who must be Luis now, I thought, but instead I asked the father "Why are you here?" There was a cautious pause, and then the shockingly incautious answer, "I work here," and the supposedly clarifying additional information: "I mean, I do regular work, I clean, you know, I don't do any of *this.*"

The hand, the *cleansing hand*—what was this? a puzzle I was supposed to solve, a surrealistic dream?—continued its work. And I felt grateful, oh, so grateful. And then I hated myself. Because from the depths of the hatred that I had tried to spare all of them so far—I had this Christian belief that hatred weakens the heart—surging forth came this mass of, self-loathing and, inexplicably, from the fiery center of it, as he finished and said, "At least you are washed now." I heard myself saying, "Thank you."

It occurs to me now that each time I have said thank you since then, and there have been many thousands probably, I could have burnt inside, but somehow, I didn't.

Through the hours, days, weeks that followed my release, through the anxious days of finding that my wife and children were safe, through the meetings, the contacts, the statements I would later give to organizations, groups, reporters, friends and family, I could tell every detail of my seizure, describe every telltale sign that might help identify my captors and lead to where I had been held and tortured. I remembered some details of the road that we had followed, I had heard train sounds when I was still outdoors, and some quite significant information about those present during torture, including nicknames. The one thing I could not speak of was Luisito's father.

I told myself that it had all been a hallucination, that it was unreal, a distortion of my memory, natural after all, because of my own hands being crushed now. I told myself that if the guerrillas got hold of Luisito's father they might do something to Luisito, who had been my patient, and certainly is completely innocent. Then I thought that someone could have put this man up to test me, that he wasn't *really* Luisito's father. Dazedly I told myself that actually this man was innocent after all, *he only worked there, regular work.* Would I not be unjust in revealing the identity of the one person who had not been a torturer?

It is now being here, in the hospital when waiting for this new operation, and hoping that if it works I may be a surgeon again one day, that I have thought about work and about life in a different way. Because I know that now, finally, there will be trials and I know that I will go to court and this time I will tell the entire truth.

I do not hate myself. That is past. But I am still ashamed.

Do I hate *him*? No, I do not hate him, I don't think so ... Not now. I hated him for my being ashamed.

So I ask myself, "What do I want? If I could send this man to prison, would I?"

I cannot quite answer that... Certainly I do not wish upon him my kind of prison, but do I really want him in prison? What would prison do for him? Do I want him punished? Removed from society? Do I think he could have done his job somewhere else and should have left that place? Could he have done that?

What do I think should happen to him?

Sometimes I have thoughts that are strange and frightening. I think he should work at some job where he could not choose what to do. Some job where he could use his skills, such as washing the lepers in a leper colony.

Yes. How sarcastic, how cruel that sounds.

Yet I mean it, in some way. And I realize that cruel idea has roots that are poignant.

Because... when I started thinking about my memory of the Malaparte story, I thought about how my mother would have felt about the story. You see, my mother used to work at a city hospital, washing patients, changing bedpans, a simple church-going aide in the little provincial town where I was born and grew up and which I left for the big city where I went to medical school. Then I went to internship and residency.

There with classmates or then colleagues, I used to be vague about her, because … I was ashamed of her.

I went back very seldom to my little town and each time I went the distance I felt between us grew greater and more definite. She didn't have any of my interests, did not understand them, didn't read, she would not even know who Malaparte was.

She never even met Susana. We had planned to go visit her together the Christmas before we got married, but she didn't emerge from the coughing spells of that winter.

So now …why did I think of the scene in the novel where the mother has kept a shameful secret? I am a child who kept his mother a secret, as if she were something shameful, because that child thought he was a great *Doctor.*

And then I kept a much worse, a really shameful secret: I protected somebody who mothered me in my shame, although protecting him might mean criminals would go unpunished.

And I do have my own punishment, in my hands, in the form of not being able to be a surgeon anymore.

But perhaps I am still a doctor, trained, as all doctors are, to tell my errors so they can help others.

So I am telling this story not only for justice to be done but for the memory of my mother and of course also for my children.

Perhaps this surgery will work, and then I will not feel punished.

And then, perhaps even my shame will fade.

WINDOWS OF NEW YORK

Imight have figured out the twins knew about it during the Thanksgiving break. They had come home a couple of days earlier, we were all busy, and I was on the phone and said something about "…they seem to happily offer glimpses into other people's bedrooms." I thought they looked at each other in that funny kind of way they have, that makes it seem as they always are complicit … But I was only half paying attention to them, as I was doing too many things at once, not just talking on the phone, but also fixing the turkey, and directing everybody to help.

Anyway, the story for me began just a few days later, at a remarkably incongruous time and place, Carnegie Hall, Oratorio Society Messiah, during the intermission.

It was Jeanne's and my "girls' night out." The habit had started almost accidentally, one time that Ted and I had tickets to the Met and he had an unexpected work emergency. Some days earlier by mere chance I had been talking to Jeanne about operas and my mixed feelings about several, which turned out to be hers also. We confessed to each other there were some we irrationally and deliriously loved, like Traviata, or Rigoletto, others the plot of which we considered horrendous, like Trovatore. In this category, we agreed, we would rather just listen to a record and try to ignore what was happening on the stage. Some we loved, sentimentally, so much, we could see live over and over again. One of those, we agreed, was Butterfly. And this evening was Butterfly! With Leontyne Price, no less! I did not hesitate, I phoned Jeanne immediately, and offered her the ticket. I actually teased her," Your older, taller sister is playing Butterfly tonight, do you by any chance want to come with me to see her?" Jeanne is very petite, but not only does she look remarkably like the great soprano, especially having the same exquisite smile, but the evening we met, we had learned that Jeanne had studied voice at Julliard.

After that, a bit timidly we thought, why not start some habit of evenings like that one? We would choose together what to do, it did not have to be cultural, it could be anything really, even something frivolous. The four of us, meaning with the husbands, we socialize, I would say, yes, we are friends, but she and I are special.

We had met them shortly after they moved into the building, to the floor below us, and their next-door neighbor invited them and us for drinks. Gradually we got closer, we had children the same age, we loved books, and music, especially music. When we were in college, my Ted had played the clarinet with a small group, and Bob and Jeanne were jazz enthusiasts. Besides, Jeanne still sang in her church, so that music quickly became an area of common interest. But it was after the Butterfly evening that we decided to organize something regular … just us chicks!

So here we were, Oratorio Society Messiah, glorious evening, we decided to have a drink during the intermission. I am not sure how it came up, perhaps Jeanne just said "So, how much of the show do you get? You are a floor higher, so your view is better but I know you often work late, so you may have missed a lot." I was totally perplexed, then she realized I did not know.

"The couple across the street," she explained. One floor below me. "The woman is always in, earlier. I think she clearly lives there. But, every single evening, almost punctually at 7, he arrives, they go to the bedroom and undress, they get into bed and proceed to…how do I describe it? Let's say, illustrate the Kama Sutra." Jeanne was laughing, her impish eyes shining, as she shared this story. They don't pull the shades? I asked. Oh no, never! In fact I am pretty sure they have no shades! "An interesting detail," she added: "he keeps his socks on." Now we both were laughing. "Perhaps it is cold in that apartment," I ventured, "perhaps the building does not have heating as good as ours."

Jeanne was puzzled. "How come you have never seen them? It's been going on for weeks. At least since October. When I invited the whole family for Thanksgiving, I was worried they would look out and see them, you know my in-laws are such puritans! —however the couple must have gone someplace else for their turkey. As a matter of fact I am not sure they are a regular couple... so much sex suggests otherwise!"

Over the next few days, indeed I was often working late, and although I smiled to myself from time to time remembering the story, I did not investigate.

However, a few weeks later, again the twins were home, now for Christmas break, and they had invited some friends for dinner. When I had just served the first course, the phone rang. Robbie got up to answer. He came back in a minute, "Mom. It's Jeanne, yes, I know, I told her we were having dinner, but she really insisted, said it will only be one minute, but it has to be right now!"

I went to the phone, unsuspecting, in fact slightly worried.

"It's on, it's on right now!" she said excitedly.

I chuckled and went back to the table. As Ted's eyebrows went up, I hesitated for a moment but then told the story.

The guests asked, "So, are we not going to watch?"

We all looked at each other, no one moved for a moment, then Robbie hurried to the switch, turned the lights off in the living room, and sure enough we all started to watch.

Ted and I tried to stay back a bit, as the kids' friends did too at first, but then they pushed to the front.

Indeed, it was unbelievable, just as Jeanne had described!

I was a bit troubled, so I tried to joke, "Well kids, did you not know it was dinner and a show this evening?" After a while of course we went back to our meal.

At the table, suddenly, I turned towards the twins, and asked, "you guys had never seen this before?"

They seemed a bit uncomfortable, then Danny seemed to blush. "Mom. What should we have done, report to you?"

He had a point!

Every New Year my younger sister, who lives in France, comes to New York with her children for a couple of weeks. She also has two boys, younger than our twins, 15 and 11. The local, older cousins told them the whole story. Of course, as soon as it got dark the younger one would turn off the lights and sit at the window for the duration!

Those two are bilingual but they communicate with each other in French.

One evening while the rest of us were in the kitchen, we heard Martin call out to his older brother, "Jean Paul, viens, viens tout suite, je t'en pris, je ne comprends pas!"

Jean Paul, who has a great sense of humor, yelled back, "Of course, that's because they are f...ing in English, you ignoramus!"

Ted and I, to mollify our consciences I suppose, decided we were greatly contributing not just to the sexual education of the younger members of the family, but also to their multicultural exposure.

The French cousins were full of questions. "Why do you think they do it always at the same time?" Robbie had an answer, "Oh, that's obvious, he must be married to someone else, tells the wife he works late. After all we don't know what happens later, he may not stay overnight. "

The business of the socks was discussed often, always quite merrily. "His feet must be very ugly" said our younger nephew. One of the twins intervened. "That is a good guess. He is very vain, I am sure, I once saw him, while waiting for her, standing in front of the long mirror on the left, naked, and he was sort of pumping up."

I did register that Robbie had a full picture of the room. But, I sighed to myself, so did all of us.

Eventually of course, the French family left us to go back home.

And the neighbors eventually put shades in their windows.

And we forgot about them.

Many months later, Ted was thinking of changing accountants for his firm.

Long ago, actually through me, he had met a woman in the finance world I knew from some benefit organization. He remembered her name, he said, Cindy, but not the last name, and recalled she seemed bright and very entrepreneurial. So I tracked her down and gave him her full name and number. When he called her she said she remembered me, remembered liking me, and also remembered we had talked about educational resources for underprivileged children. Ted thought she sounded interesting and indeed very knowledgeable. Over the next couple of weeks they had several phone conversations. The talks turned to something more ambitious, not just for Ted finding a good accountant but also using profits for some social cause in a way that would also present a tax advantage. There were many complicated aspects, but she was very kind and accommodating of Ted's crazy schedule. Actually, both their day schedules were hectic, so she said, why don't you two come over for a drink and we'll talk details, we will include my husband who is a lawyer, he will add a perspective we do not have.

Ted agreed, and they fixed the date, some relatively early evening on a Saturday.

On the evening in question we looked, for the first time, at the address which she had emailed him. We then looked at each other. No, it could not possibly be, it must be the building next to it, I said with faint hope. As we crossed the street we started to be more certain, and more disturbed. "She" I started, knowing we both remembered her very vaguely, "she had long hair before-right? But …her… general outline… it could be." We vacillated. There is nothing we can do now, we agreed.

It would be our punishment I mumbled. As we pressed the floor I sighed, it fits, it fits.

The elevator opened directly onto the apartment. They ushered us in, warm and friendly. We sat in the living room—yes, the same living room where we had seen him come in, always at 7 PM, and after kissing her, start undressing—and they served us drinks. At some point when the conversation unexpectedly turned to Manhattan real estate, they excitedly told us that they had recently purchased the apartment for a more than reasonable price, there was some long story about that, and in that context they insisted in giving us a complete tour. Already from the moment we had entered the place Ted and I had avoided looking at each other but now, during the tour of the bedroom which we knew especially well, we were so rigidly avoiding each other's eyes that I started to have neck cramps.

To any unsuspecting observer the evening would have looked quite pleasant.

As we crossed the street to go back to our place, we felt totally dejected. We were silent at first, but of course we already knew the outcome of the encounter. The non-outcome rather. "I cannot have any business dealings with her, with them," Ted said. "I cannot. I don't see how I could. I have to find some excuse."

How did you leave it with her? I asked. I had been talking to her husband and missed the last part of the exchange. Ted sighed, "I said I would consult with my partners and get back to her. "

But he did not.

He did not consult, and he left her a brief evasive message, surely outside working hours.

Months passed.

Again my sister and her children came to visit.

The encounter is always joyful as all of us are very close. And especially because we are partly a French family, food is central.

I had made a spectacular meal, and I had announced it— well, almost all of it —by email and by phone, well in advance. So it was a topic already before their arrival. From the moment they came in and starting unpacking, the dinner was the central exciting subject. My famous shrimp and ham roll, my orange and mustard glazed pork chops, my surprise dessert. The twins of course knew it but delighted themselves in teasing the cousins.

Then, in the middle of dinner, Martin, our younger nephew suddenly asked "So, what is happening with the couple across the street?" He had barely finished the question when Ted and I ferociously barked in unison "That is a completely inappropriate question!" We followed with some other vehement, critical comments.

The boys' parents looked at us in utter amazement, so we rapidly toned our response down, and made some moralistically stained statement that must have sounded bizarre.

It was not until later in the evening, once the kids were gone to watch TV, that we told the story to my sister and brother-in-law.

We laughed, but our discomfort did not subside. My sister asked Ted, do you see her, do you see him at all, either of them, professionally, in any context? Yes, Ted sighed, sometimes at a financial event. And? my sister asked. Ted said: We nod at each other, obviously a bit uncomfortably.

Well, among other details, obviously, I added, we never reciprocated their gracious invitation. At best, it all seemed puzzling to them.

We all wondered, could we have done anything differently?

My brother-in-law said, "You should have been smarter and figured it out right away from the address."

And then what? I asked.

You could have found some excuse right away to not go ahead with the business plans.

We considered this retroactive suggestion. How would that have been better? I insisted.

My sister asked Ted, would it have been really totally impossible to go ahead with the project?

For me, yes it would, he answered, for instance, we could not have socialized with them. I certainly couldn't Don't you see our voyeurism weighed on our conscience?

We all looked at each other.

Sadly, we agreed, there was never a chance for an easy solution.

Since they knew Jeanne's role in our involvement they asked if I had told her the story.

Well, I confessed, once when Jeanne mentioned them, first I barked at her as ferociously as we both did earlier at Martin. And then I told her what had happened.

And assured her that through me she would never meet these people socially!!

Jeanne is my accomplice in many things I said. I am sure… well, I hope rather, that as we grow older, we'll chuckle from time to time remembering.

But. I wondered … what is the moral of the story?

Does the story have a moral?

It occasionally has crossed my mind, though that concern is peripheral, if we missed something important we might have gained, in terms of the business issues.

Mostly, I wonder, did we …look bad in the children's eyes?

Actually, worse, DO we look bad in their eyes?

Would we act differently now?

I asked Jeanne that question, knowing that I was putting her on the spot.

Look, she said smiling, being Black makes me very aware of the potential for negative perceptions from people, including some people in our building as you very well know. The idea that Blacks are a bit perverse I guess. And, as you also well know, I once was in analysis SO: I do think about these issues from every angle. At least I try to.

That evening at Carnegie Hall, when I told you what was going on, we were having fun. I shared with you something that was unusual, very definitely unusual! And certainly, a lot of fun. It was not even a great secret, remember? You didn't yet know it but several neighbors had been talking about it.

I did not expect you to have a moralizing response. And you didn't have it. There was a playfulness in us, something we always share, it was like suddenly being teenagers. We have chatted about how we were always, both of us, very good girls. So this was… definitely a break from the usual… We were being a bit defiant of our own rules.

You are not asking me to apologize for perhaps having indirectly messed up some potential business deal for Ted, are you? I know you are not.

So.. the moral of the story…For us or for them?

I looked at Jeanne in amazement. You are being provocative, I said.

No, no, Jeanne answered. I am being …extremely reasonable! You see, something I learned in my analysis, voyeurism is almost always problematic for most of us… but exhibitionism is acceptable, socially acceptable. Don't you watch TV, read magazines, don't you see the generation of our own kids?

Actually, she added, the moral of the story is ONLY for them!

This is it: "If you want to be nice to your neighbors, DO pull the shades closed when you are having sex!"

ACKNOWLEDGEMENTS

This book owes a lot to Loren Schwartz, who carefully and lovingly edited my stories.

Not only did she humorously comment on my "British use of commas," she also nudged me to be bolder with some knotty plot issues, shared her emotions as she read the stories one by one, and patiently listened to all my doubts about the order in which they should appear.

Very special thanks to Gabriela Aberastury for her art and for her generosity.

I also want to thank Arnie Richards for his confidence in me, and for his valuable teaching during the times of The American Psychoanalyst. Also Matthew Bach for suggesting other, new literary paths, which I hope to explore in the future.

Finally, thanks to all the friends and family who over the years read fragments of these stories as they were slowly being developed.